Matvey Silkin is a Philosophy & Economics undergraduate at the London School of Economics. His passion for writing grows from his reading of the classics as a younger child, along with scientific explorations as a teenager. His passion for writing started from a young age, being published in a poetry anthology, along experimenting with various writing projects when younger. This is his first full literary work in the form of a novel. He aims to use literature as a way of studying human nature, doing philosophy and developing empathy. Matvey's other interests include spirituality, the arts, sciences and health and fitness.

To my family for challenging my assumptions about the world, sacrificing so much to raise me and for the love that they offer every day.

Matvey Silkin

GARDEN CITY

AUSTIN MACAULEY PUBLISHERS™
LONDON • CAMBRIDGE • NEW YORK • SHARJAH

Copyright © Matvey Silkin 2021

The right of Matvey Silkin to be identified as author of this work has been asserted by the author in accordance with section 77 and 78 of the Copyright, Designs and Patents Act 1988.

All rights reserved. No part of this publication may be reproduced, stored in a retrieval system, or transmitted in any form or by any means, electronic, mechanical, photocopying, recording, or otherwise, without the prior permission of the publishers.

Any person who commits any unauthorized act in relation to this publication may be liable to criminal prosecution and civil claims for damages.

This is a work of fiction. Names, characters, businesses, places, events, locales, and incidents are either the products of the author's imagination or used in a fictitious manner. Any resemblance to actual persons, living or dead, or actual events is purely coincidental.

A CIP catalogue record for this title is available from the British Library.

ISBN 9781398403369 (Paperback)
ISBN 9781398403376 (ePub e-book)

www.austinmacauley.com

First Published 2021
Austin Macauley Publishers Ltd
Level 37, Office 37.15, 1 Canada Square
Canary Wharf
London
E14 5AA

I would like to thank Austin Macaulay for the publication of my book. I would like to extend my gratitude to many of the teachers and coaches (formal or not) I had for expanding my knowledge about the world and helping me build my character in the process. I would like to thank my friends (you know who you are!) for the enlightening conversations that we have and for helping me realise that there are many perspectives on our world. Finally, my family for the reasons that I describe above and for that beyond words.

1

Occasionally, there were moments in my life that I could not discern if they were a dream or not. Nor could I describe them, being clear that some things were not easily reducible to words. We remain alien to one another, to a great extent, because we cannot express, adequately, the complex tapestry of Feeling and Consciousness. This is the essential moral problem. We have base words such as anger, joy, fear, but these do not account for the complex composition such sensations have. No one can measure one emotion and thought over another. And hence value one over the other, which is why ethics is unscientific and relies solely on the abstract tools of intuition.

Recurring memories dominated my thoughts, and I could not understand if they were illusory. As time stretches on, illusions and reality solely coalesce, becoming nothing more than an image. Thus, memories were unreliable, and dreamlike. Dreams were a fantastical arena, and I analysed them as much as I could, for they gain insights into reality that were inaccessible in the waking day and sported much value. They were an exciting playground for the Irrational and a means of self-awareness. Freud said that dreams told us what we really wanted, and such a fact was undeniable. If I remembered, I could always link what I dreamt to something that I had desired, or feared. If not both.

I reviewed last night's events. I imagined myself sleeping, and waking up and illuminated by the pallid street lights outside, a clod of hair gently appeared. Followed by a sharp nose and a comical face. The face was whitened to highlight the deadpan nature of the face. I panted under pressure and my arms tensed. I was ready to fight. My head became heavy with fright. 'Relax…' the face eased. A submitted smile, the reality and warmth of it in the eyes.

'What?' I murmured.

'I am who you think I am.' I started to slowly contemplate who this odd man was. The lightly olive complexion, but svelte nose gave him away as French, the familiarity was striking.

'No, well, I am René Descartes.' The man's smile quickly turned into a frown, expecting some excessive politesse from me. It seemed disingenuous, the eyes caverns of anguish. It was interesting. People tended to do the opposite, feigning pleasure, not frustration. Such deeds tended to be within mockery's domain, but I relented out of respect for the great. And out of fear in case this man was a lunatic in my room. In life, one had to consider all reasonable possibilities, however disturbing. Indeed, I kept imagining this very moment in my head years before. Not with Descartes, but with any random person.

Watching the movies made me obsessed with the heroic and I craved the excitement of that kind of a life. But yes, it had its cost.

'*Monsieur, pourquoi vous êtes ici?*' I deigned, gesturing respect to the great.

'No, please, let me oblige, let us speak in English, I have to practise my tongues.' He licked his lips, almost relishing his cheeky turn of phrase.

'Sir, why have you come to me? What is it that you wish to inform me of?'

Descartes eagerly climbed in, and yawned, flailing his arms around in order to stretch, and sat crosslegged on the floor. His brow furrowed and he whispered,

'I wish to gift truth.'

'Could I get you some Fanta?' I asked.

'What is this Fanta? I have quite plenty of phantasms every day, thank you very much!' My bathos must have been an annoyance.

'Get a man some water, will you!'

He banged the floor so hard that my coat, in fact, fell off!

'Yes, sir.'

I plodded along to the bottle and gently blinked my eyes out of their lethargic state. I desperately scrambled for a mug to use for Descartes, checking each one for cleanliness. I went to the sink and started pouring water.

'No, no, no: there will be cholera! Do you have a pouch or some kind of bottle?'

I opened my cupboard and then handed Descartes a plastic one. He gently stroked the texture and was confused.

'Well, if it is nothing else, and not from the tap, then it is satisfactory. A corkscrew?'

'Just twist the lid, sir.'

Descartes aggressively tugged the bottle cap and I twisted it to the side for him.

He poured the water down his gullet. 'You see, the problem with you moderns is that you lack respect for us and you are so alien that it is difficult to imagine us as part of the same species.'

'Perhaps, but we are what you will become.'

Descartes rose, storming out of the room. I tried to reach for him, stop him going into the real outside world, but then the sight of my room dissolved into nothingness, and I saw then the whites of my eyes, with a passion of colours dancing next to them.

It seems at that moment that I woke up and I became utterly confused at. I made sure that my window was closed each day and my coat hung firmly on the metallic hook.

What I had seen and observed was no less real than ordinary life, but the sheer implausibility of such a situation was enough to dissuade me from belief. After all, man is flawed, man may be wrong, and things ought to be approached with reason.

I rushed outside the room to see if the philosopher was still walking down the stairs. I heard the crashing of steps, fast such that someone was running. The room looked as it did in the dream, and the coat was on the floor, and the window was swung wide open. The particularly fascinating thing was that my room was still warm; the cold early March air insufficient in making me feel uncomfortable. I slammed the window shut and shook the coat from its dust. I sneezed, and a cloud of dust erupted from my mouth, illuminated by the dimming moonlight outside. I gazed in wonder at the delicate and gentle effluence of the particles out of my mouth. The beauty of the world arose from a really close observation of various aspects of reality and putting them into an appropriate perspective.

My mind shifted back to this dream. It was far too vivid, even though there was a radical incongruence. The room also seemed to look the way Descartes had left it. Still, there were a myriad other explanations, like an action by me when I was not awake. In the stuffy university rooms, it was perfectly plausible that I opened the window and knocked down my coat. The vividness of this dream was interesting, though. Yes, I was self-aware, but not to the extent of remembering all of my dreams. The events of last night were surreal, but for fear of being dragged into pointless thinking, I assumed that all that happened was a dream. Not certain, but clearly a supposition that was good enough for now. I rammed the papers into my satchel, frustrated at the creases.

The desk was covered in a flurry of papers, such that I had to spend several minutes each day mining out what was necessary to be found. Most who came inside pointed it out, but I always had a reason, I was too busy, working on a project, I was distracted. Artful procrastination. I had rooted myself in the assumption that I did not need to change, and even when I acknowledged this, I had a reason that would help me ease out of responsibility.

2

The young scarce honour the wise. As children, we are born excessively overconfident, and that without an older, more experienced, helping hand, we are sometimes faced with arduous challenges. An inability to achieve makes us ashamed of our constant efforts and we sometimes flag. Effort is never sufficient, we need an intelligence, along with integrity such that we can labour with knowledge. I used to think every failure was down to a case of stupidity – which on reflection, appeared the case.

I used to believe that: but now I'm not so naïve. Reducing things to generalities tends not be effective. Much more so, how a thought was phrased is of far greater importance than its content. Even if one sports folly, what is the glory in pointing it out!

People shroud themselves in excuses, putting their failures down to tragedies of circumstance, the system. The fact is that, however, some people have managed to do what once has failed to do, so ability must be lacking. And when one is not able, it is because one does not know or simply lacks character to do it. So, when we fail, we are all idiots in one way or another. It is not appropriate to label one an idiot, however, as we are nothing more than our actions' summation, and it is not really clear when persistent action becomes a part of our respective personalities. However, this shift in understanding, of course, will happen at some point to us.

That is why I committed to make rational thought a key part of daily life, holding reason as supreme. My fascination with the concept almost bordered on something of the obsessional and religious, such that I never questioned it. A paradox. For without it or without God, nothing was right, and once one deviates from the sure path, we tend to be led even further from it. I knew that I needed to believe something without a doubt, and the fixed creeds of reason and God permitted such an audacious act.

That is why every waking moment that I had free, free of others, free of potential burdens, I spent pursuing for more insight about the world. Looking at books, looking at others. For although the other judged and knew us by its unnerving gaze, we could do the same, creating equality of respect. As we feared the other, the other feared us.

As such, knowledge was obviously something of supreme value, and a teacher was to be respected at all costs, without exception. Having a teacher was something that extended beyond a contractual formality of capitalism. Contracts alienated us, making us separate from the sacred relationship that the giver and receiver of knowledge possessed: the teacher-student connection extends beyond the pecuniary. A teacher is to always be respected and listened to, and a student must always be taught. However, for this to persist, one must ensure that both do their duty and fulfil their roles adequately.

It is a kind of friendship, for, among the great intellectuals, teacher and pupils were always friends, although never equals.

It is with this in mind that I entered a discussion with my teacher on reality. It was a question that had always fascinated me, for everything had to proceed from the real. If our thoughts about the world were falsities, then there would be no point in thought. For thought aligned our actions in accordance with reality, slowly etching the patterns and unities of experience within.

'So, Gabriel, what do you think is real?' Mr Jansen inquired.

We met in a different place each day, and I decided that a café was the best place for today's proceeding to be held. Any great thinker had to have a place designated for thought, as the existentialists had their Parisian cafés, the Greeks had their lycée, the pandits had their mandirs. It was deceitful to suggest that thinking was only of our own accord, a place also had to be conducive to the very process. Sometimes we were only the products of our environments. Places became infused with an associative spirit, which spurred on further achievements in the field desired. It became habit.

The reason I loved cafés for such intellectual discussions was that they were festivals of the senses, where sights and smells danced in harmony, and one could make apt connections between ideas and concepts, and reason too. However, the presence of such profundities may have not been appropriate in places where people went to relax, which is why I intuited a quietening around us, and muttering in hushed tones, in reaction to what was said. We were ruffling a bit of feathers, so what, we had the right to speak without overt offence. The flâneurs were immersed in their habitat, ready to punch at any opportunity to trivialise the complexity of our lives and provide fodder for their fiction.

While I considered the happenings around me, I thought about what to say. Time was valuable for both of us, so I decided to be precise in what exactly I had said.

For a moment, I indulged in the image of a cylinder extending in both directions to infinity, consisting of endless instants. On inspecting these, one would enter a new universe, without leaving the first.

'I think that the reality is everything that is perceived,' I retorted.

Jansen tilted his head back up, gazing at the ceiling above.

'Do you agree with me that there can only be one reality?' Jansen replied. 'It would seem that there is only one way that things can be the case.'

'I would not necessarily agree, there is only one way in which things are, but everyone sees them differently.'

'Exactly, but it must be conceivable that there is one true state of things, but there are different perspectives, not all of which may be correct.'

'So the reality is truth?'

'Yes, Gabriel, but the truth is not as simple as you try to gesture. Things may happen, and their happenings may be true, but not really exist. The question I will leave you upon is, are dreams part of our reality?'

I hesitated and stared at the baristas preparing the coffee for the hungry customers.

'I guess they are. I mean, there is a reason why they came about.'

'Then, how do we know what to trust?'

'Hmmm… I guess it's to do with the intensity of feeling, the apparent nature, and coherence.'

'See you next week.'

Jansen was a fantastic teacher, for he knew that the essence of knowledge was couldn't just be expressed in sentences, but that there also was a mysterious element that ranged beyond it, ineffable and inexplicable. It was ultimately beyond human language and could only be expressed in gestures, contexts and feeling, entities so complex that it was impossible to appropriately articulate them and for the Other to also fully apprehend them. Some principles had to be meditated on, similar to the activity of the Zen master Hakuin Zenji, who persistently contemplated the koans his teacher bestowed to him.

Finding that there was more than one legitimate way to view the world, when both opposites were true and equally so, created a form of omnism – a freedom when anyone could choose as a belief what they liked. And there was solace in that.

Learning had to somehow have the perfect balance between independence and assistance, and I found that Jansen managed to present this balance well. Organisation and industry were above talent in the grand hierarchy of virtue, which is why I was an ardent adherent of the principles of scientific management. Taylorism was one of the ideas that made the modern, capitalist economy. As these ideas could be applied to firms, so could they to individuals, making my productivity skyrocket. Only the daydreamers viewed life as a journey; what is done must primarily have a purpose.

Wanderers will err, and get lost.

3

I quickly learnt that life ought to be lived by grasping and paying attention to each moment, and the rest of the matter was in mind. Moments of pleasure had to be amplified by one's mental faculties. As Buddhist monks can warm themselves up in freezing cold, so can a human control their body.

The miracles that religion tout are not always acts of God, but incredible instances of what each human being can achieve, with proper training and thought. It is no wonder that there was something about the human condition that was truly divine, and admirable, a core that resided in every human being. It was a lie that there were no limits to our performance, but the limits of man are far beyond the immediately imaginable.

One of the great pleasures of this world is food and is something that we should really be thankful for. The Christian tradition of saying grace before one's meals is testimony to that and is a most justifiable action. You never throw away food because another almost always lacks it. For most of human history, food was something of the utmost concern, dominating daily life, but now is something even seen as pure necessity. The amount of individuals that grumble at the idea of cooking dinner is astounding when it is a laudable skill to whip up a spaghetti Bolognese or craft a smoothie. I believe that people take a too shallow an attitude to such a crucial aspect of their lives. A dietician for me was a necessity, and luckily the university had one, so my eating could be aligned with what was available.

I also wondered about the ethics of eating. Were animals allowed to be eaten? Did they have sentience? Even the scientists did not have answers to these questions, and it seems like I would be forced to choose an approach. I did not have an answer, so I would put the dilemma away, and let experience offer me a verdict on its own accord. It was an interesting idea posited to me by the vegans that I knew. And the passion with which they argued it was compelling. The idea of one world and one species was too much to ignore, and an appeal was contained in the unity of nature.

Sometimes I ate with friends. And sometimes I ate at alone, willingly. Too often, I overlooked the beauty of eating, and it was at moments of solitude that I really came to understand its value. My friends didn't really understand why I did this, finding my rejoicing in solitude quite odd and unusual. A friend said that I had a weird tendency to spiritualise things, and he likely pointed it out from an arrogance. Whatever, some people just don't get me.

I guess it was contradictory that I did not believe in God, but often engaged in introspective activity. I guess I understood how things really worked, maybe the pious and I spoke of the same thing – but I saw it for what it really was.

Today I had a beautiful cuttlefish risotto, the obsidian ink fascinating, and I sat in the corner so that no one could throw me off my rite. I loaded the fork with rice, added a bit of the squid on top of it, and let the food slowly slide into my mouth. The firm, tender flesh of the squid, allowed me to exercise my teeth and gradually feel the juices flowing out of it. Talk about pleasures of the flesh. Masticating the food made me feel part of something greater, a cog in the Universe's eternal system of composition and division forever and ever more. I swallowed the chunks and let them glide gently down the gullet. The unconscious work of the stomach would do the rest. As for the rice, however, the starchy nature of it made processing a battle. The more I chewed, the more the rice would still together. I brought the rice around my lips and teeth, feeling the texture, and swallowed as well. For though it was delightful, the process went on and on. The metronomic monotony slowly pulled me into a state of blissful nothingness. I always left time for a moment of thought, and either stared at the fields outside or observed the people within. Both were extraordinary ways of learning about the world, each revealing insights to be treasured forever. So a system had to be built so these memories could stay in mind forever and others could gently leave the realm of consciousness. The mind and body were a temple, and by definition, only the good could persist there.

I rose from the table and slowed walked to put my tray away. Even with my rucksack, I felt unusually light, and that was a sign that all was well. It was a convenient summation of mood and physical health, and I had to value the moment. For the sea of life was calm, but only for a moment. Storms come and go, and one must be vigilant for their presence.

It surprised how shallow a look on life others sported. There seemed to be no depth in their perception of the world and the beautiful interconnectivity of everything. For, in a way, that seemed to be the hallmark of true intelligence, an inference of one principle from others and competing facets of evidence. It took me some time to realise that it was not just a depth of knowledge that was important, but also a breadth. Understanding the infinite complexity of anything was an intense source of pleasure, not only through its intrinsic goodness but also for the utility that proffered in aspects of our lives.

I did believe in a transcendent world beyond us, a kind of realm of the Forms. It was clear that our perception was limited and that only reference to something external to us, ie God or pure ideas could everything in life be justified and adequately explained. The world did not reduce to fundamental particles; there were byproducts (such as love and goodness) that could not be expressed by a materialistic lens. Those who denied their existence or rebuked their invocation were heartless.

4

At my age, it was of the utmost importance to have another half. I never believed that two lovers were destined for each other, I thought love was something conditional, at least romantically, and that it was something to be won. There was a reason why love and war had no rules; these were both battles that defined the very existence of all participants involved.

For me, love involved the willingness to be ready to die for something. And I thought that I could never have that for another person. People were too flawed and seeing people's drawbacks so apparently made it hard for me to sacrifice much to them.

There was a reason why hopeless romantics had that very nature, they waited for destiny to take its action, and kept in that eternal trap via their misunderstanding that good things come to those who wait. Strategies must be crafted; actions must be taken, for pleasant things seldom emerge independently. However, in any task, deception is of the utmost importance as well, to make everything done seem enchanting, and away from the profane. I never lied; I could not bear the harm that they could bring. I experienced a revulsion at hearing lies; knowing the lack of truth could bring a worldly ugliness that was difficult to revoke.

But deceit was a different category because actions were based on interpretation, not a set meaning. So using actions to trick was somehow less reprehensible than the use of words, although consequences also played a part in determining the rightness of the action. The determinant of morality was rarely something clear.

The beautiful thing about Laura and I was that everything was so effortless. I could never quite understand why. She was sporty, athletic, had a fantastic physique, whereas the longest distance I'd ever run was a few yards away from an angry neighbour. Opposites seem to attract. I distrust seductive beauties, throughout history using their looks to disarm and obtain their goals. But I looked at myself, and there was nothing she could take away from me. Sure, it was apparent that I had looks to charm, but I didn't have much else in life. So, I trusted her, and our conversations then always went in real deep after that.

We met up each day in the cafeteria for tea. We could not stay for the whole day as we then had parties to go to, but we spent so much time together, and I can tell you that these were some of the happiest moments of my life as such.

'Hey, beautiful.' Our lips touched, we rubbed noses and sat down. The grip of her arm was strong, and that was endearing, showing a mixture of intimacy and vitality from her. Nothing was missing nor superfluous, and that is where the beauty was.

These matters were art, and the masters had an intuitive understanding of these cues and performed them to perfection. The moves were not made with any conscious effort, the artificial seeming genuine.

I looked at Laura shaking the protein shake. Her arms compressed, the strain showing clearly. She then started to take a sip, and as she lifted the cup, her relaxed biceps turned into large blocks, decorated with arteries. It was a beautiful witnessing of biomechanics, how people can move and look brilliant. She was strong, no doubt, and I felt like she excelled as an athlete and a personality as well. I sometimes wondered if I really loved her, as opposed to the idea that she embodied. It was a complicated question, as we rarely desire a person for their essence, as opposed to the positive qualities they contain. Our judgements mask themselves behind an objective standard, whereas we really try to mine what is necessary for us.

I guess it really depended on if I was ready to accept her imperfections. And due to their intensity, that was not always an easy question to answer.

'How was your day?'

'Yeah, it was fine. Nothing much happened though. How was gym?'

'It was great! I think I'm hitting personal bests. I could do ten deadlifts for 100k.'

'Wow, you're getting really strong.' I put my hand on her arm and pressed gently. It was weathered tough with years of training. I like the virtues that these emphasised in a woman, dedication and resilience.

'All right, don't get too intimate with me! You complain about nothing happening, you should join me.'

'Of course, you know, if a ball hits me, I might just shatter into pieces!'

We both giggled at the thought of that. But she persisted: 'But seriously, I'm quite worried about your health. (*What!*) You might not live past 30, for God's sake! Think about it, we might only have five more years together…' she sighed.

I tilted my head forward and looked into her eyes. I wanted to say something direct and assertive, but I couldn't. The wide dark depths of her pupils lured me in, and I was flustered as usual.

'I don't think you should worry so much about me,' tilting my head to the side. 'But you are right.'

I realised at that moment that it was obvious, I loved her, which was a really dangerous thing. Somehow, I managed to frame all of her flaws in a positive light, which frightened me. Maybe, that is what love really was, an acceptance of everything somebody throws at you.

I realised the danger that a relationship like that could present to the future. But I was tired of thinking about the future. It was time to enjoy the present moment and to stop contemplating potential eventualities.

What we enjoyed in our relationship was the ability to talk constantly to each other and directly. There was no clear communication barrier it would seem, and that was the basis for the time well spent together.

'Should we look at the stars together?'

'Let's do it,' I said. 'Then we walked out of the cafeteria, wrapping ourselves in the coats that we had.'

'A roof is a beautiful place this time of day,' I said.

'Yes, especially when no one is there,' she susurrated.

5

I could not emphasise how privileged I felt to live in a city where it was possible to gaze at the stars without the lights polluting the view of the sky above.

In reality, I felt a complete lack of emotion on observing the heavens above. So many others spoke effusively about the wonder it had filled them with, but I just found it a part of nature. What was so great about them? They were just a part of nature, like any other object. No one goes around gasping when they see a cat or a tree, so why do the same for some stars? I thought that maybe I should have more empathy for my surroundings, be more feeling as a person. But I was perfectly happy with the way that I was. Being emotional all the time was a burden. It was really better to keep a cool head on my pair of shoulders.

'What do you think?' she said.

'I think they're nice,' I answered. 'What's so remarkable about them, though? I mean they're pretty, but so what?'

'For some, it's how big the Universe is,' she retorted. 'But for me it's just the fact that there could be other life there. You know, just like us, but instead, looking in the opposite direction. Isn't that brilliant?'

I paused for a minute and believed in that idea entirely. Because if you think about it, there probably were aliens out there. The Drake equation dictates it. The universe has trillions of stars, and most of them are eliminated by their respective planets not having water and being away from the habitable zone. Much of the remainder would be lifeless, with the civilizations within never forming or pettily pushing themselves into oblivion.

'I guess it is pretty nice,' I replied. 'Imagine if they came here right this second...' I envisaged a UFO coming down right this second, with its beam shining upon us.

'That's pretty silly,' she replied.

'Why? I know they're out there...' I responded.

'It's unrealistic.'

'I'm sure the government would know.'

And she sniggered slowly into silence.

'I love how you think differently to me,' she said. Looking at other couples, I knew there would be a problem, not a benefit.

'I'm tired,' she murmured. It was time to wrap things up for the day. So, we held hands and walked down the staircase. I do feel a rush of desire, flowing through my blood. I always wondered what love really was; whether it was something spiritual or purely carnal. The theorists said it was both, but I knew one would suffice. The cold winter air augmented our warmth for one another, feeling an attraction stronger than ever before. I wondered if she felt it too, as strongly as I did. I knew I was intense and felt more strongly than anyone else. I feared this relationship would end and remembered a film that I saw when I was younger. I wasted years of my life as a youth, looking for the answers to questions which had none.

'A relationship is like a shark, it's got to keep moving forward, or it dies.' That's what Woody Allen said. A filmic childhood provided a lot of answers to these profound questions.

Did we have a dead shark? When we were alone, we entered these semi-awkward, semi-profound silences. Still, it felt like we were becoming more and more spiritually intimate than ever before. We still didn't have any fun together, though. She was so beautiful but always kept me at arm's length, because of her religion. Hebrews 13:1, 1 Corinthians 6:19-20, etc.

I researched it all and she was still right. I admired her principles. I grew to love her personality, but the truth is that I primarily liked her for the looks that she possessed.

It seemed like an actual romance that could occur kept being delayed or annulled. I almost believed that she was toying with me. The inherent romance of the night sky was too obvious, it was either a subtle game she was playing, or she just didn't pick up these things. It was disturbing to contemplate. I left her at the entrance to the building, afraid of crossing a threshold into awkwardness.

I sighed and gripped my shirt, creating a little tear. It was a nice metaphor for the effect of all this on my psyche. Freud said that the lust for love was as strong as the one for violence, and I empathised. My face scrunched up as I walked back to the roof.

I looked away at the buildings, the little houses, peppered with the glitter of light. This was the start of something new, a burgeoning feeling of vitality in this city.

I looked below, and I saw the abyss. The radical darkness of it was alluring. Throwing a pen down, I heard it hit the ground. Satisfied, I walked away.

***

Bad day at uni, then? Jack wondered.

'No, it's Laura,' I replied.

'What now?' Jack questioned.

I questioned whether I gave too much. Our friendship often didn't seem equal, for a lot of time was full of me whining on about my problems. That could not be good for a long-term friendship. He wasn't some kind of a tool for me to use.

'You know what, enough about me, it's irrelevant, how's your job in the upper echelons of power, then?'

He sniggered and then replied, 'Well, not there yet, but that's the eventual aim!'

'What exactly are you working on at the moment then?'

'Let's talk about it over some pool.'

6

Pool was a great activity. It allowed one to stay and chat a bit longer than a drink. I rejoiced in the self-awareness that I had without alcohol, happy that I did not abnegate what I felt, and would unlikely do something that I would regret.

There was also the benefit of being away from the rest of the pub, as such actually being able to have a proper conversation. Looking at the lads there, a few years younger than me, but often seeming to lack a generation's worth of maturity. At around nine in the evening, a watershed occurred, and slowly an aura of toxic masculinity seeped into the surroundings. What began as a lighthearted series of jokes would descend into swearing and ruffianism, eventually degenerating into violence or worse. Looking at the evolution of people's gestures, I fast learned the right time to leave these places.

In addition, most of it stunk. It was intoxicating, slowly luring everyone in the surroundings to a collective insanity.

Unusually, no one was there to use the table. That was one of the benefits of a fledgling town, everyone had more space to themselves, and if something was shared, you tended to get it.

I placed the triangle to the side.

'So, what are you really doing, then?' I asked.

'We're working on an exciting project; we're basically planning the new residential areas of the town.'

'So, like architecture?'

'No, what we're doing is laying out the water and electricity grids, and then the building companies buy the greenfield land off from us. Then, they'll most likely build high-rise buildings to the side of it.'

'I thought this was like meant to be a green area, low rise, very eco-friendly.'

He struck the balls, potting a few. 'Yes…yeah, but there's restrictions about building materials and the city overall's going to have a negative carbon footprint.

Your turn.'

'But you going to keep the fields on the city outskirts? It's great for walking and the like.'

'Look, I've been keen on keeping the garden city like that as well, and I can't tell you too much. But they want to make it into agricultural land, as there's been miles unused here for millennia, and you know the farmers are struggling at the moment. Look, the Service is going to do the minimum to classify this as a city, but no more. The Service is keen on restoring the accounts this year. We're doing all we can to get the National Debt down.'

Something didn't seem quite right. He was being far too factual, and actually a bit of a bore. He started being less of the role model that he once was and looked needy. He fiddled with his hands a lot. I remember in the debating club about a decade ago, he was the leader who taught me to speak up for myself and make my views heard. This guy taught me courage and respect, yet although he was my friend, over time, he started to become a grumbling middle-aged man. I knew that I'd have to say something to bring him to light, although I had to be extra careful in my choice of words. Failing to help a friend in need scars relationships permanently, as I learnt through hundreds of mistakes with others.

'I want a beer,' he murmured. He slammed the door shut and blasely strode off into the distance. The young girls slowly gave way. He did look nice. He had a wide frame, really tall and his skin looked clean. Their feet pointed towards him, and he placed his arms on his hips.

'One pint, please.' He tensed into a smile, while the ladies observed. His eyes were dead inside, and he gazed longingly at the drinks piled up at the back.

He came back into the room, smiling and sipped.

'So, what's happening between you and Laura then?' he inquired.

'You know, it's all going a bit slowly,' I replied. I tried to phrase the situation delicately.

'There's no sense of progress you mean?' he was leading me on.

'I mean, look, we're having great chats and spending a lot of time together. But we're not really getting any more intimate, and now she wants me to meet her father tomorrow.

It's confusing and a lot of pressure.'

'Well, you can't just say no, can you?' He paused before finishing the question.

'Yeah, but apart from that, I've really got to figure out what to do next. This is all really confusing.'

He nodded, affirming that I was listened to, while being wise enough not to actually offer me advice.

'How's the baby doing?' I gently nudged his shoulder.

'She's doing well, growing up to be a strong girl, like her mum.'

'And Jen?'

'She's doing fine! But I don't want to talk about that. Right, we've got to focus on this game then, haven't we? Looks like I'm going to win again then.'

He thrust the cue brutally into the black ball, and it thundered into the hole. He raised his arms triumphantly and looked to the sky. He gave out a burst of laughter.

'Clear up then,' he shouted. He sat and waited for me on the couch while I cleaned up.

He looked at the floor, whilst I put the equipment in place. We were finished, and I stood at the entrance.

'How's work, really then?' I inquired.

He shouted, 'Look, I don't really want to talk about it. It's too stressful. I can't really talk about it much. But you're a good friend for asking.'

'We're here for each other,' and he nodded along.

'Come on, let's go,' he smiled and shook hands and parted.

Wilde said that there were two tragedies in life: not getting what you wanted and getting what you wanted. It is kind of self-evident statement, in that these are the only two possibilities when someone desires something. Of course, there are cases when we partly get what we desire. Somehow, I thought Jack was the latter.

But today's conversation seemed largely odd to me. He didn't share anything about his own wife, and he kept asking me about Laura. They did both know each other. I started to get suspicious, but it was the first time that I entertained such a possibility. Still, he was a wheeler-dealer political type, and I knew from the news that they had a tendency for such things. Nonetheless, I dismissed it. Whether it was wise to do so is another matter.

7

I knew that certain rules did need to be followed to attain certain things, but an adherence too eager was a cause for concern. Sometimes rules did need to be broken in order to achieve a greater good.

Rules were really manifestations of principles, abstract innate human values that were cherished. That idea would solve most ethical dilemmas.

Religion used to remedy this, saying that God protects the good or rewards them with an eternal pleasure in the afterlife. The epitome of reason, love and will would be sure to fulfil this.

But there is no necessity for this to be more than a figment of the imagination. It could just be an idealisation of human virtues – and not an entity separate from ourselves. With no God, how do we know what the future exactly holds and whether our good deeds will be rewarded and worthwhile? These emotions dominated my chest as I advanced to Mr Mércier's house.

The man lived in a beautiful neighbourhood, the hedges saying who land was whose. The houses were white, with the walls of some engraved with beautiful decorations of times long gone. A civilisation's art arguably possessed the most in historical truth, simultaneously revealing its heroism, thoughts and dreams. The place reeked with yearning to this past golden age, an island of civilisation in an otherwise barbarous city.

The streets were clean, the place well-tended. The condition of road signs tended to be an indication of the kind of people who lived there.

This was the area of the high-flying intelligentsia and politicians; they pumped money in to ensure that the area was as safe as can be for them.

I counted down the numbers and glanced at my watch. I had found my way to the Mércier house, Number 23. I was unusually early and had found my way well. The house was pink, and the gated driveway protected the realm within. Ornate spikes guarded the walls, and I immediately realised that this house could not have been inhabited by a man with security. The flowers stood tall in the earth, and the sprinkler oscillated up and down, spraying water. I decided to sit in a nearby park and relax before this mission.

It was two and a half hours here from Cookton, but such travels were necessary. It was high time that I met the Mércier family. It was a mutual examination. Looking at how my two sides of the family interacted, I often thought, did I really want to be with one group of people for the rest of my life? These people could make it brilliant or terrible, and I had to accept them as I accepted Laura. The people in these places could be real caricatures, but the overall situation was no laughing matter.

It mattered too much to be trivialised. So, although the train journey was a slog for a country boy like myself, it was worth it. I was lucky to have a Home Counties accent, so I could convince this family that I was more well off than I was. These families look for class and the wealth that validates it.

For me to have planned love in the family was also an aberration: remembering how my parents met. 'Twas a case of instant love at first sight, or what science calls De Clerambault's. My father was smitten the moment he met her, and in all places, at her place of work. She was a midwife, and yes, my father was the client. She was delivering my half-brother, Tony, three years prior to when I was born, and my father cried at the sight of seeing his first son in delight. Of course, he didn't love my mother more than he loved Tony, but the connection of events seemed too strong to be ignored. My mother constantly argued with my father that he did not really love her for such a reason. The strange thing, however, was the view Tony took of the whole matter. He never showed us any disrespect or hatred; he treats all of us as one of his own! I am surprised that he showed more maturity about this than any of the adults in our complex family tree, but maybe that just shows experience does not always make us all the wiser. Maybe, love was not something to be fought for, but to be gently received from what life gave us. The capitalist spirit was mythology in many ways; good things did not always come to those who grafted for them. Indeed, striving for goals may lead us the wrong way, if we lack the tranquillity to clarify our purpose.

In many ways, patience was a virtue over industry. So, what I was doing could be in vain. But, seeing it as part of life's grand adventure, I could confidently say that I did not mind this experience.

I was not sure whether there was value in planning for the future when enormous turns of fortune like my parents' could easily occur. The future was so uncertain; sometimes, I thought it would just be better to live out the day, and see what each offers independently. For all we know, we could be thinking most unclearly at this very moment, our judgement corrupted beyond our control. Everything seemed so much clear in a different state of mind, so maybe one just has to wait until one emerges upon that level, and then make their decision then. I wanted to see how others thought in these same cases and maybe draw from their insight or experience. Sometimes I so desperately wanted to find out the thoughts of others that I let out an intense stare at them and listened to their words as hard as I possibly could. Some were enchanted, but others were put off. If only I knew what they really thought if only I knew what they were really going to say. The process that I would have to embark would become exponentially easier.

However, I understood that maybe now, it was essential to come in relaxed, and empty the mind of thoughts. Focus on the here and now and let the rest take care of itself. I pressed the doorbell, and it rang. As the rain knocked desperately on the pavement outside, I pressed the doorbell and tried to relax, focussing on the first impression. Time lengthened and I would have to take action at any possible moment.

8

Steps neared the door, and I saw a figure in a white shirt nearing me. The door creeped open.

'Hello, you must be Gabriel?' the man enquired, as I observed to understand him and enter his thoughts.

'Yes, sir,' I replied, offering my hand and then feeling the full force of his shake. The pain entered my ligaments, and I was forced to submit, frozen in the moment's intensity.

'Please, call me Mr Mércier,' he answered, and I was offered in. I slowly sauntered around this impressive home, with high ceilings and all the signs of riches, and was ushered into the dining room. The whole firm was at their tables. Mércier's wife, another lady, Laura's younger brother around the rectangular table. They were all sat, ready for dinner, and a maid stood at the ready to serve the first course. I had the feeling that all of this was a large test, and beyond the nervous smile, I felt dreadfully ill at ease.

'Hello, everybody, I do hope I'm not late,' I laughed.

'You're not, please sit.' A little tyke pulled out the chair, and I sat: this must have been Laura's younger brother.

The formality of the occasion was daunting; all of the ladies' donning dresses and all of the males wearing suits. I wondered whether this was all an elaborate test towards me, as nothing seemed to be geared to making me feel at ease. The faces of those around the table looked sullen by ennui, weathered by the force of paternal authority. Still, they seemed blissfully content, warmed from within by what seemed to be a strong family unit and material comforts. I started to think about why Laura did not talk about her family much. Did I want to be a part of such a family, even if my wife would be wonderful?

Everything in this world had a price; the real question was size.

'Laura tells us you're pescatarian, so we've prepared a fish dish for all of us to enjoy. It is a trademark cod in wine sauce with pasta.'

'Sounds delicious.'

The little tyke next to me asked, 'So why do you only eat fish then?' I waited and assumed that the parents would tell him off for such a high degree of opprobrium, only to find them waiting for an answer. I had respect for the boy's audacity though.

'Well, I think fish do not have the same level of consciousness as mammals and birds, which are the other main types of animals that we eat. Their nervous systems are too simple for them to feel any pain or pleasure, contrary to their higher counterparts.'

'What about bugs? They're stupid too.'

'No, they don't taste good,' I said laughing along.

My giggles were like voices shouting in the wilderness. My mind zoomed out, and I looked at the floor and imagined a giant tumbleweed rolling along. I had been detaching myself from my senses less and less recently, but in unusual moments, these feelings came back to me. The family's humourlessness showed a gritty realism: something humanity's great thinkers had, a dose of honesty about their thought. For the first level of honesty was not lying, the second was speaking one's truth as precisely as possible. This too required the ability to do so without having to offend or threaten oneself.

This place of sternness started to feel likeable.

The servants brought out the food piping hot, and the steam from the fish seared into my face. The sensation was beautiful, and I warmed.

Mr Merciér raised a glass and uttered, 'I propose a toast to our guest.'

'To our guest,' the table answered in ensemble and raised their glasses thus as well. This man had a fearsome control upon the house, although one that was also worthy of respect. Some tyrannical wannabes failed in their oppressive task; this fine man somehow found a way to enforce his will.

The wife croaked, 'So, how are you enjoying university then?'

'It's all right; I love what we're learning, but, you know, between yourselves and me, there just isn't that much to do there. I mean, it's great for walks and thinking and that kind of stuff, but it gets tiring. We are quite focussed on our work though.'

Laura interjected, 'But it is an exciting environment: we get to see real time how the future is being built.'

The wife replied. 'That's the thing with new cities, especially garden cities. They're kind of a halfway house. There's just enough people to feel cramped, but not enough services to have stuff to do there. No wonder they abandoned the idea last century.'

I entered.'I found it an unusual scheme – it's all part of that movement to win back green votes. It's a real issue.'

Mr Mércier placed down his cutlery, asking, 'What is your politics then?'

'As a management student, I think business must be protected and that there is a good working culture.'

Mércier sniggered, 'You one of these tax-big, spend-big types then,' and the child sniggered in turn. He really did seem to take on the sins of the father, and was close to a diminutive version of him, both in appearance and personality.

'Not really. Actually, employee satisfaction tends to be measured more in terms of Kreuzberg's hygiene factors and aspects of the workplace itself and the associated family life, rather than salary, although it is by no means a minor component. Stuff like company culture. It explains why big bankers are always unhappy, while someone like a baker has a great life.'

'The rich do earn their own misery, it's true.' Mr. Mércier looked out of the window, as if he remembered something from the far past. There was a pause in anticipation. 'We're not having a full dinner, by the way, just the main course.' Mércier pointed his thumb at the door towards the maids. The taste of rice entered my mind, as I finished the last pastas on my plate.

'You can leave,' he told the family, and they briskly paced away. The chairs clattered away and the servants respectfully went to their places. It was like an evacuation for a typhoon, or at least the preparations for one.

'As you can see,' Mr Mércier continued, 'I'd like to have a chat with you one on one and outline some of the expectations that I have surrounding my daughter. You seem quite polished, and able to converse about some topics with great fluency, but I need to know that you're not a scoundrel, like some of Laura's previous suitors.' He coughed slightly.

'Dad, not now!' Laura shouted, clearly being in earshot of her father's candour.

'Laura, please leave…' Mr. Mércier replied, and Laura went away. He continued in the following manner.

'Apologies. Now, I need to know if you have a good academic and humanist's brain, alongside the moral integrity that it brings. I am so glad that you do not do pure science, of course, psychology is not one! The natural scientists fail to capture life's essence in their worldview, being so far detached from pure human experience.'

I related to what this man said on some level and decided to listen in further.

'Tea in the Library?' I accepted and conceded that this man was not as one-dimensional and authoritarian as had first appeared, and I was determined to discover more.

9

'What are you interested in?' Mr Mércier retorted. 'What makes your eyes burn with fire?

What do you love?'

'Sir, you're asking all these strong questions, I don't quite know how to answer!'

'You must think about ideas in your spare time.'

'I guess I'm interested in becoming the best version of myself. My life is kind of one extended growth mindset. I intend to fulfil my potential.'

'That is a very mature way of looking at things.'

'Well, life is short, and I feel like we have to learn something while we're here and also enjoy it. Hence, not a single moment can be wasted. It's worth it, I gather. The thing I fear most is the long lingering feeling of regret. One always knows that they themselves are to blame for it on some level.'

Mércier tilted his head up to the beautiful chandelier above.

'What about yourself, Mr Mércier?'

'I have always been enchanted by one enigma. Other people. They are fascinating beyond all reason and could be the greatest mystery of them all. We know so much about the

heavens above, the atoms below, and the most existential questions of all frankly have no answer! A man can know all this, and still, be a complete mystery to oneself. Never mind others.'

I hummed in agreement.

Mércier continued, 'I do things that I do not know why I do. And it frightens me, for I must know why I do certain things. The horrors of the world are rarely committed ex nihilo; rather there is a slow march there, although often blithe and invisible. For then, I am truly free from myself; I cannot restrain myself, and the future becomes even more uncertain.' He took a deep breath.

'And it becomes even harder with other people.'

'That's true, I look at you, and you appear to be one thing. But how do I know that you are not completely the opposite, and a charming deceiver?'

'I can assure you I'm not!' I joked. Instead, he smiled in agreement and journeyed on in his speech.

'There are cavities of unknowns in the middle of each other human being, and it is largely impossible to disentangle them. This complexity is beautiful, and ones sees even in the most miserable and tragic wretch, the potential somewhere, someday to be happy.

And I must help them. That's why I'm a psychoanalyst.'

I dug further, 'When did you find this out?'

'You know, you read about all these prophets having these epiphanies in front of burning bushes or in distant caves. Some call it psychosis. And this sometimes happens. But my core beliefs were formed in them months reading these very volumes and trying to understand the world through this. The meaning of any life begins from some kind of belief or passion. We live in a world of desires, and human history is written on the masquerade of our personal wishes as universal.'

'Knowing or not,' I said as I nodded along. I gazed at the ancient volumes on the shelves.

'May I?'

'Please.' I stepped towards the volumes and glanced at the titles there. I discovered that I was sitting next to a true humanist. In modernity, this was becoming rare, with people eschewing the scholarly life or instead, simply opting for tribalism, becoming the pen-soldiers of a political agenda.

The volumes of Freud and Jung clothed the library; there was a Dostoevsky and some Nietzsche. It explained the house's 19th century décor; here was a man who tried to live in the past, and occupy a historical niche that brought him the greatest satisfaction possible.

'Do you prefer Freud or Jung yourself more?' I wanted to explore if he knew about the degree of influence that he had on his children.

'Both actually. Freud's model of the psyche is compelling, but excessively environmental. Jung is right to point out the existence of a collective unconscious. We do seem to store certain symbols of the world within us, which overall make an impact upon us. To a great extent, what we see is determined by perception.'

The door slightly creaked, and I slowly tilted my head thither. A black feline beast occurred, and I resisted the impulse to cross my fingers, and they twitched resisting the impulse.

'Come here, Melchior.' The cat sprinted across to Mr Mércier, leaping up into his lap.

I felt as if I was inside a genius' lair, augmented especially so by the sight of him stroking the creature. The cat was an esoteric creature, more so than the open and energetic dog, and even after looking it in the eyes, one could never really decipher its nature.

'There, there,' he said. I looked in Mércier eyes, the pupils neither dilated nor contracted even as he looked into the distance. The cat started to jump off and scampered off, giving me an aggressive glance with his emerald eyes.

'He's off. That reminds me, I've got to put Lucas to sleep myself. If you would excuse me.'

I'm sorry about Lucas earlier. He's a blighter, that's for sure, but he means well. He's one of those testing types. It's never good to subdue that instinct in children; often, they've got to fight their way through society.'

I inflated my lip and agreed, 'Assertiveness is a very desirable trait.'

'Yeah, but you'll learn at my age it's important to keep a bit of a leash on them as well.

That's our role as fathers, be disciplinarian and someone to love them. Tough love.'

He left.

I lay down on the sofa, trying to observe the library in higher resolutions of detail. The world map wallpaper was alluring, adding to the room's rustic sense of appeal. I had to sit up; in case I had become overly familiar with the place. I noticed how I had started to sink into the cushions there. It reminded me of my childhood, in my grandparents' house, next to the fire… Although the places of our childhood could not always be accessed, they have a strong place in our hearts, and by analogy to what we see now. The books inside provided a comfortable shelter inside the library, a bulwark against what could be a turbulent world outside.

I heard gentle footsteps down the stairs. I loved how by listening closely, one could know who was coming, without having to see them.

'Hey,' Laura came in.

'Hey.'

'You survived?'

'Yeah. It was fun.'

'Very gushing, eh?'

'Yeah, I enjoyed the conversation! I have to say, your dad is really clever!'

'I know, but it sometimes means you can't really talk about other stuff…'

'Maybe, I've never got that with my parents.' I stared blankly into the distance for a bit. 'Do you like where you lived? I mean area wise. Your street is quite calm, but everywhere else is pretty hectic.'

She sat down on the sofa. 'It's fine. It gets a bit noisy during the day, but there's always lots to do.'

'The big city has both costs and benefits.' I looked out from the window, and could see, even in the darkness around, that the leafy landscape was more rural than Cookton.

I heard the gentle clatter of car keys: 'I'll take you two to the station then?'

'Let's go,' Laura said.

'You drive then?' Mr Mercier asked.

'No, not really.'

'Not even in a rural area like Cookton?'

'It's small and it's like one big university park. Buses take us to any place worth visiting.'

'What about the future?'

'You know ten years, driverless cars, and no one will have to. Why bother learning now when it will all be useless?'

'It's like chasing the wind.'

I looked outside and thought, *how the area would look in ten years?* From the experience of childhood, ten years tended not to be enough to revolutionise a place completely, but history had certain periods of change that tended to be more accelerated than other epochs.

We were at the station, and even at ten at night, a steady stream of people was emerging from within. That was the thing about big cities like these, they never slept. It would be good if they could stop once in a while, it would be better for everyone's health.

'Well then, it was a pleasure meeting you, Gabriel. Let us meet again soon.'

'An honour, sir.' I leant forward and outstretched the open palm for a handshake. I understood this man's immense force and had to respect him.

I looked back as we entered the train and had a strong feeling that this day would be imprinted on my psyche, forever.

I met my lover's parents; I was breaking new ground.

10

There is this experiment called a Rorschach Test which presents the subject with several inkblots, and they are meant to show their thinking patterns, by somehow analysing it and describing it. I first met it on a trip to the school nurse. It was primary school, and we were talking about a poem together and what it made us feel. Personal, but still very boring. I knew why I hated the literature of primary school; it was full of the mundane, bears in woods, fairies, dragons. Who cares? That's not the world we live in, and even a five-year-old understands that. A book has to be a message to the world in some sense. So, I went to the nurse, and she showed me these weird inkblots, which were meant to look like something: apparently a bat or a flower. I just started talking of the flavours that I tasted in my mouth and the gentle sounds that I heard. I was confirmed not psychotic or under the influence of narcotics. But I was instantly branded with some sort of condition as if my thoughts were not normal. What was normal? Diversity, if not to the harm of self or others, should be treasured. People come from all different backgrounds, but surely it is more right to treasure the different ways in which the mind can function, rather than our origins? All this psychological research is based on a scientific worldview system rejecting the spiritual, only based on the countless studies of rich Westerners. How dare we nurse our values above others?

The systems of oppression that the elite used, whoever they were, were deeply ingrained in the science we used. The gun is not enough to thwart resistance; an internal prison is thrusted upon the oppressed, a panopticon of the mind. I'm not saying that I was, although my parents kept moaning about their fortunes and the rich and powerful. Growing up with little money can leave these kinds of marks.

Perhaps the only reason some mental states are branded aberrant is because of their potentially negative effects. Sometimes, I experienced a kind of sensory overstimulation and needed to recollect myself. A place to wander and to passively experience the diversity and wonder of life was sufficient. The supermarket was one of them; it was a festival of life, and all sorts of fascinating characters walked through its wide and towering aisles.

It was surprising how the entirety of someone's existence could be summarised. You could see all these people walking through, the snivelling scroungers, the high-fliers, and immediately you could judge them. It was moral arrogance, but for me, it just seemed like there was no way of living without concluding something about another people. It was about survival, not necessarily ill will.

I looked at the fruit and carefully inspected the apples, testing each of them for quality.

The bumps on their fragile skins were symbols of authenticity, but sometimes I would rather eat something that was fake and tasty, rather than real but ugly. That's what many think about truth; they want something that is a sham but appeals to the senses. I was taken back to my childhood and remembered the days when I was out in the supermarket with my grandfather. I realised the immense value of these moments too late, and I wish that I would have been more respectful during them, but unfortunately, we are blind to the truth at times when we are younger.

To say I was someone who lacked focus was a brutal understatement at best. My mind always wandered, and I started to contemplate things totally irrelevant to the moment. It was safe to say that I was someone who lived in the future or the past, but never the present. That way, I missed out on the intense joy that moments could create. As I walked to the till I eyed the faces of those passing us. The micro expressions on their faces sported the secrets of their lives, and it was my job to uncover them. Real power was finding people's secrets.

I walked outside into the mall and travelled up the escalator, walking past the rest to the top. I caught sight of the bookshop at the top and wanted to have a look.

There was a café on the side there as well. I saw some classmates. Normally, I would come and then have a chat, but I felt that I needed some time for myself.

I felt like that I needed to spend time on the creation of some things; I felt this insatiable force within me, urging me to take action in this world. Such a mighty thing could not be stopped, only channelled outward. To prevent this force becoming a mighty vortex inside me, I had to create. For when the powerful keep their waves of energy to themselves, only they themselves are destroyed. I took a peek through the window, and a beautiful young lady greeted me. She was red-haired, bespectacled, in a turquoise dress.

'Sorry, we're closing.' My eye twitched. I felt a connection.

'That's fine, I'll come tomorrow,' I replied. I did.

11

Immortality was the aim. Ever since I heard about death when I was six, I've always looked for ways to evade it, even deride it. It was always a core part of my vocabulary when I was a child, but you only realise its awful horror when a loved one dies. A way to deal with the meaninglessness is to create, so that is what I did. My preferred art form was fine art itself. Nishida said that the artist describes reality more accurately than the scholar. The scholar assumes to argue, the artist speculates over nothing, he states what is perceived.

I decided to preserve the unique experiences I sometimes had by taking up painting. I was not interested in painting portraits or landscapes, as I believe that we see more or less the same thing when this happens. But thoughts, dreams, the only person who knows what you saw is you; and even that can be supremely valuable. That is how Mendeleev conceived the Periodic Table; Einstein refined his theories; these events are evidence of the interplay between creativity and hard logic. So painting was a hobby of mine, and splattering someone else with paint was joyful. I gazed at the model in concentration. She was half-naked but as defenceless as if she was completely so.

This is psychologically legitimate: indeed, Freud's theory of sublimation encourages that this must be the case. A way of fighting our whims was to somehow redirect them to something more socially acceptable. I could model my ideal woman and fall in love with her accordingly.

I went to the art shop again. There was a little blues riff playing in the background, prompting me to stroll in as a satisfied customer. I eyed the canvases, dreaming, hopefully, one day I could create something like that. There was a rack full of brushes, and I stroked the gentle tips. I saw some movement in the background. It was her.

'Hi,' she whispered, placing her hands on her hips, thrusting them forward. 'Can I help?'

I was confused.

I tilted my head, looked her in the eyes, and eased out, 'Painting supplies, that's what I'm looking for.'

'Painting supplies?'

'Yeah, what about them?'

'They're right there.'

I put my head behind my neck and scratched my head. 'I know, but I'm looking for books about them. You know to learn. I'm not a born El Greco.'

'Of course. This way.' She let out a sigh, too short to suggest frustration, too long to suggest glee.

The tomes were covered in a flashy covering, glossy to appeal to the kitschy youth.

'There. Anything else?'

'Not yet.'

'OK, if there's anything, please ask.' She flicked her hair back. I smiled back, as well. Did this woman like me? I was taken, but the attention around flattered me.

She liked me. This girl likes me. Her name tag said 'Alice'. The eyes told the truth in everything, and I looked in the mirror. What did this girl see in me? I was dressed in a beige bohemian coat and purple trousers. Nothing particularly appealing. Then again, people have different preferences.

I bought the paints and brushes that I needed and returned to the apartment. I took out a sheet of painting card and then started gently applying strokes of paint. The paper was dominated by fine lines, and I tried to replicate a scene from my dreams. The waves of the water broke over a purple boat and fire erupted from the depths of the sea. This ambiguity made me want to gift it to Laura. She would like it.

Some women like handbags. Others like expensive holidays. Laura did. But she had a thing for art, and in her apartment, the walls were donned by these diverse items from across the world. She sent me photos with her friends, going to galleries and looking at all these unique items. This was capitalism's solution to the desire for heterogeneity and uniqueness in areas of our lives. Workers experienced alienation from the output they had produced, and there is a strong desire to feel ownership. The working man's fruit is taken by the capitalist, who brashly sells it onto the highest bidder.

'Thank you so much.' She kissed me. I played a game with anyone I had the pleasure to kiss. I tried to be the last one to pull away and see how long we could go. I had to know. But slowly, Laura's face was turning into something else. I tore off.

'Are you OK?' she asked.

'Yeah,' I replied, and I thought I was telling the truth. 'I'm going into the kitchen.' What I had seen was the prelude to some sort of a nightmare, the moment when the enemy is about to kill you, when you realise the falling person off the cliff is you, hitting the ground at any moment. She was Alice, her face invaded my mind. An uncontrollable neurosis that one could not resist. I had always felt a tingle of attraction towards Laura, but nothing as strong. I breathed and said that this would pass.

12

Perhaps, I was deluded. Maybe, this whole Alice thing was something that I made up because I felt pretty bored most of the time. Things were going overall well, and that was dull. I thought that before when happy. I needed another perspective, and after a drink with Jack, I decided to have a look around. She was in for her Saturday shift, and we entered the shop separately.

'Hey, what you looking for today?'

'Colouring pencils.'

'Sure, I'll take you with me.'

'OK, thanks.'

I stroked the pencils for a minute and headed out to the exit.

We walked in single file out of the shop and far, far away from sight.

'What on Earth do you think you're doing?' Jack interjected.

'I just wanted to get some supplies, that's all.'

'Don't give me that! I can see her seducing you. She's after supplies, all right.'

'Yeah, you're right. I wanted a second opinion from someone who I can trust. I've been suspecting her pulling the moves on me, but I'm not very good at seeing.'

'Yeah, you're not. Joking man, you've actually gotten better.' He let out a laugh, but then his face morphed into a stony expression.

'Never go into that shop again.' Now I had to return. 'Something bad is going on already, I can feel it; don't make it any worse by spending time with that lady. She could ruin your life as it is.' My eyes darted around, and I nodded. Jack took a deep breath.

Intuition was powerful, often neglected by the society that we inhabited.

'Laura is a nice girl. A brilliant one. Out of your league. And this girl is trying to get in your heart. Well, that's gonna ruin everything you worked for.' He gesticulated with his hands, looking for some other formula inside.

'You want to have someone to value, and not just cycling through all these random women. Because these days don't always last, and we've got a duty to protect them.' His fingers started stroking up and down his nose and water started seething at the surface of his eyes.

'Are you all right?' I had to ask.

'Things have been tough recently. Jen is kind of getting really aloof, we're arguing a lot, a wage freeze has been introduced, and he just keeps coming onto me, again and again.'

'What do you mean, coming on?'

'He's relentless, he just wants more drawings, more designs and it's hard to take. He doesn't care about any of us.

He just wants his promotion, and it doesn't matter to him that we'll be ten years sooner in the grave.'

'What have you done about it?'

'I don't know; I just don't know what to do…'

'Tell me what you want to. I'm here for you.'

I'm glad he listened, and we did, in fact, have a discussion. He did feel better after. It was just a lot of grumbling and dissatisfaction. I walked him to the bus stop and let him go.

I thought about whether to take his advice on board. The art shop was the only one in Cookton. Really, however, there was no issue; I could just buy some stuff online. But I did not like the relentless march of the digital; it eroded real human experience. I could visit the shop and not have to engage with this girl. I'm also sure Jack was exaggerating, he was in a mood, and even when he was all right, he had a penchant for the melodramatic. He was right; some people had to be told to their face to back off. I went in.

'Gabe, you're back!'

I stretched out my neck and stood up straight.

'Alice, I know where everything is.'

'Can I come with you?' She offered her hand.

I froze; I did not know at all what to do. Everyone was looking at us (or so, it seemed) and I accepted. I shuddered briefly while doing so.

My stomach tensed and blood rushed in. It was that heavy feeling of immorality, knowing that you had crossed a line. I had committed adultery of the heart; and I quaked, knowing I did wrong.

'Are you not painting this week?' Alice asked.

'Painting is the only thing I've been doing these past few months. I want to try something slightly different.'

'There's a new art show in Birmingham, do you want to come along?'

'With whom?'

'Just us two?'

'Listen, Alice: I'm sorry but I can't do that. I have a partner already, so I don't think I can be going places with you alone.'

'Why didn't you tell me?'

'You know, it's not something you mention out of the blue. But you are very nice.'

Alice paused and understood. She let go.

I paid her at the till, and left in silence.

Laura had to know about what I did; I wondered if she would mind. Hard moments in our life emerge, and we must address them. We can face them now, quashing them, or wither and be overridden.

13

Fear is something that is ultimately instilled by the environments around us. Some of us are more sensitive, but the way that this sensitivity is applied differs, case to case.

It went far beyond that. The word only has power when supported by wrath and its corresponding might. My brother and I only had the courage to conduct mischief when we were away from any adults; their faces seemed austerely authoritarian. The treatment of our father hardened us; the childlike smiles were mechanically excised from us. He was violent, but had self-control. One laugh out of place, one mistake, it all came to back to the belt. One lash and we returned into a state of solemn seriousness. Its black serpentine nature kept coming back in my sleep; and some days, I saw the very make, with the logo, crawling in the grass at night.

Cookton, in comparison, seemed paradisical. The place was infused with youthful energy and the corresponding optimism that arose from it. It was enjoyable to lie down in the long blades of grass, with the moisture of the ground refreshingly pressing against my shirt.

Either way, as I lay, I was inspired. The vastness of the blue or at times white sky above me was humbling, the muddy ground below fascinating. The unity of creation was apparent.

It wasn't always peaceful, but the turbulence of the world around us arguably only made it even more stunning. Apart from the clusters of dark woods in the distance, this place was as close to its status as it was when mammoths roamed the Earth.

Ten years was not enough for a place to be fully transformed, and Cookton was little older than a year. The town was a massive building site, and the sea of concrete sprawled into the grasslands around. There were animal safety professionals removing the adders in the field, even though a bite was rare, and poisoning impossible.

Men had a tyranny unto the Earth, often subduing it. The prerequisite for any kind of rights was not an inherent dignity, but a propensity to bite back. The adder could not en masse, and neither could the other flora and fauna in the environment.

I don't know why Jack was here. In London, he'd be a city boy with a secure job, but no, he went to this Midlands outpost. Being a civil servant was tough, and the pay meagre if you did not try and compete with the rest, so promotion was essential if he wanted to make this policymaking a proper way of life. He was a budding architect when younger, and I often caught him drawing buildings and seeking to improve them in some way, whether that was via design or making them more cost efficient. Amidst the wonder of being left astray in the wilderness, it was clear that town planning was a job for him.

The landscape before was decorated with cairns and tors, but this was contrary to the system that the developers had in place.

In a way, urbanisation had a similar destructive effect on the mind, via the parallel of education. The landscape, as the mind, is slowly cultivated for the exploitation of the elite, and its unique features are stamped out. The result is a machine, an uncreative one, processing the output of the world blindly and without essential thought. Many of the successful had the ability to think powerfully deductively, but not do so laterally. A school was the start of the employee culture, where supreme discipline and obedience to a superior was required, and punctuality and inflexible rules were enforced.

The greats in this world were rebels, people who challenged the order and the status quo and bravely stepped out into the unknown. They went into the woods, battled the mysteries inside and emerged, victorious. They were the embodiment of the Booker's quest plot. Exploration was a rehashing of the society within. In a way, there were no objective maps; they were all methods of relations that we created for ourselves. We create our own stories and our own geographies. I was a staunch postmodernist in that sense. Given enough scrutiny, all categories tend to fall apart and then everything is revealed as a figment of the mind. It all came down to a feeling. Justified or not, I did not really know.

14

I rang the doorbell, rapping my feet in anticipation. My feet played out a jig, and I shuffled around. As I heard footsteps towards the door, I straightened myself up. I patted down my blazer and fixed my shirt. My feet slowly jittered around as I saw Laura stop. It was late at night, so understandably, she was wary before opening the door. The door bulged out as she leant in. The door flashed wide open, and one foot of hers stood right next to the door. The leg was plump, venous and had a rosy hue, and bulged out beside it.

She tilted her head, 'My gentleman caller.'

I looked up at the ceiling briefly and uttered, 'My lady.'

'What brings you here today, fair traveller?' she said, raising an eyebrow. Blood flowed through me, and I had to hold myself back.

'Nourishment, for the body and the heart,' swinging my head out, and winking back.

'A fair request.' I walked in and we hugged each other.

'What happened today then?' she was very good at reading subconscious gestures and the nervous rapid contraction and relaxation of my muscles obviously offered a hint.

Her tone of voice changed, gently rising up all the time in expectation. It was depressing to see that I could not be straight, even with the closest person in my life.

'It's the art shop. I can't go there anymore.'

'Why not? It's still open as far as I know.'

'Yeah, but it's the people there.'

'What about them?'

'There's this new shopping assistant who gets on my nerves. She keeps trying to get intimate with me.'

'And?'

'She keeps flirting and trying to hold my hand.'

'Did she hold your hand?'

'Yes.'

'You let her?'

'I felt like I couldn't say no. Everyone was watching me.'

'Gabe, that shop is empty most of the day. Artists are weird people, they're too busy engrossed, looking at the materials.'

'OK, whatever!' I exclaimed, aware that I was rationalising a bit. 'The point is I'm not going there anymore and that's that. But I know I'll go mad without art.'

'Just buy online, the shops are gonna close soon anyway. It's cheaper there.'

'Yeah, perhaps. I know what brands work for me anyway.'

And I thought this little story in my life was over. How wrong I was.

15

She was incensed by the newspaper article.

'This whole anti-God thing: it is the worst thing to come out of these times. You know it justifies all sorts of horrid things. People say that religion is horrible, but you know, no God is worse. Look at all the horrible things that are being done outside!'

She was overreacting once again, portraying the world in an extremist language.

'Without God, there is no right or wrong. It all descends into mere opinion.'

She might have been right if morals were just about rules. But it's not like that – rules are too inflexible to be universal, and right and wrong is more about principles. We have to discover universal values among humanity, whether bestowed by emotion, nature or God, if he exists. Then we must use all our creativity to obtain these virtues. Still, this discussion was for another time.

'I'm sorry I questioned your beliefs. It was wrong of me, and I don't know why you believe what you believe, and the other thoughts and experiences that fuel this predicament.'

And I really meant it. There was no point in lying about feelings to other people; one could see straight through that.

'Look, I should have just said that I didn't want to; that would have been simpler for all of us. Religion is a controversial topic.'

I interjected. 'Oh no, religion should be discussed, as we're a couple. However, it should be done more effectively.'

I paused. 'Well, I think the bath's ready.'

'It's fine, I just want to escape a bit,' and she turned on the TV. The news was on and as usual, it was a panoply of flashing images of conflict, destitution and lies. I had a firm reason to believe that the media was one of the reasons for the negativity and discord in the world. When the bad is highlighted, it grows. It is a way of filling up our minds with pseudo-intellectual garbage to keep us occupied. It is a food, consumed repeatedly, but there is little retained.

I walked into the bathroom and closed the door, but I did not shut it. I diligently hung up my clothes on the door, on the hook, away from the wet floor, and saw the shameful figure of my body in the mirror. Too much hair, a small layer of fat, a few rashes.

It was imperfect. But it was really me in an unauthentic form. Clothes were a great equaliser, and they made one feel beautiful on the outside.

I put my arms around the bathtub and slowly dipped myself in. The water sloshed and foamed as I immersed, and I rested my head on a cushion at the end of the tub to maximise my comfort levels. The scents coming from the deep underwater below soothed my reason, and I entered a trancelike state. I took the duck that normally stood on the grille next to her bed and let it swim. It was great to loosen inhibitions and once more be a child.

There was no point living up to an ideal, in private, which one did not believe in.

Torrents of laughter elided from the living room. Laura seemed to have changed the channel to something funnier and more cheerful. It's true: the idea of these spa breaks and weekends was over-romanticised. The initial feeling of relaxation is transcended by a certain apathy. It moves into a compulsion, where you feel a necessity to use what is already there to get your worth, although there is no innate inclination towards it. I just felt like listening to her, finding out more and drawing some insights from my thought myself.

I did not know why I always brooded over things like this. Ever since I was a child, I wanted to dissect ideas, draw conclusions, meditate on things, until reality gifted Truth. I was never someone to accept things as they were; I always sought to find a way to get what I wanted. Perfectionism. Others took things in their stead and just proceeded on with life. I wondered why I was possessed by ideas like this. Was this something to be accepted or battled? People were essentially different, and it was a long and painful process for one to become like another.

Laura was laughing. That told me something. It was easy to split the people in our lives between the humorous and the serious. The humorous point of view is well known; it is good to laugh because it is inherently pleasurable. The serious point of view is seldom promoted. I tried not to be funny, not because I wished misery on me or anyone around me, but because I viewed it a lie. I could not do what I truly did not believe. So, I tried to substitute the constant hunger for pleasure via intimacy, and not humour.

I lay down on the sofa beside her. I stroked her arm.

'Going to bed soon?'

'Yeah, it's late. Intense day in the operating theatre tomorrow.'

'Yeah, they never really make us rest, do they?'

'Hm.'

My body felt lethargic, and I dragged myself up from the sofa into a sitting position. A moment ago, my face was planted in the cracks of the sofa's cushions. The smell was good; it must have been new. I blinked myself awake, and the light made my eyes water, hurting. I gazed into the mirror ahead and saw their crimson shading ahead. The body spoke the truth, but it was manifested in a million different ways.

We both rose and hugged. We kissed. I tried to hold, but let her go. I was unhappy. She was. I often dreamt of their figure in my sleep, holding her, so close. I only wanted to conquer her once, but she ended up conquering me. There were many other beautiful women I could have, what happened today showed this. Was I being stupid?

I noticed how I was idealising her, exaggerating her positive features when away, but in here, I saw some of the worse features she possessed. Slobby, shallow and stubborn. Would I really want to spend the rest of my life with that? I started to regret my thoughts, but denial could only make things worse.

I used to think that viewing everything via the mechanism of rose-tinted glasses was the solution to all the ills in this world, but now I knew that it was a cause of them to a great extent. A healthy dose of realism manages to cure many troubles.

16

Laura invited me to have a look at her gym during the following week. She told me that I needed to get more into the sport and explore ways to stay fit. There were recesses of this university that were not properly explored, and this gym area was one of them. Academic grandeur morphed into a kitschiness infused with body odours. This, in its very architecture, seemed to be a place that did not value nuance and agility, but rather one that prided itself on force, functionality and simplicity. Ideologies were not products of the mind, but rather elements that arose from the actions that we completed.

Blocks of muscle and bone walked past me, inadvertently or deliberately barging past me in the narrow gym hallway. I could not understand why these people could live such a monotonic life, full of the same painful routine, day in and day out until some vestige of a result would emerge. They may have lived longer and been more successful in some sense of the world, but the mundanity of their whole lives was not worth the extra time lived.

The gym was two-tier, and as crammed as could possibly be. Weight racks were stacked back-to-back, and the air was stuffy. There was a rowing and running machine at the back, and the rubbery floor was wet with the water that careless gymgoers had split. The peoples of today lacked a religion, and godless people all over the world flocked into these obsessional rituals to find the belonging that our age's greatest thinkers had torn apart. The future is not necessarily better than the past, and we ignore the latter's lessons at our peril.

It was so dangerous to go against the values of the societies which we lived in, for a view out of place could often cost somebody their life. There was a mundanity involved in following the crowd, but the boring things we did ensured our survival until their regularity numbed aversion to them. We had to brush our teeth, which was a cost in time, but we did it anyway. The question which dominated my young life was, whether I should fight to defend my identity or do as the Romans in Rome. After all, selves were impermanent, and being inflexible with it was like chasing the wind.

However, I knew that men should not become who they did not want to be. I did not enjoy the masculine culture that these aggressive activities possessed. I knew that there was no escape from these negative side-effects, so I stayed away from much of the sporting activities. They teach you to press on, go in pursuit of a goal despite the storm. However, no one is perfectly resilient, and eventually, you learn to stay away. It's a catch-22.

I did envy them to a certain extent and remembered Dostoevsky's work. 'The intelligent man could not seriously become anything, that only a fool could become something.' Or something similar. People needed an obsession, faith to achieve something. Having no doubt was the reserve of the ignorant, and courage could scarcely be justified by reason. It is the will to continue that pushes people on, rather than indifference to their fear.

The powerful had an air of simplicity about them, imitating particular archetypes, and adequately emulating the role that their job demanded. They feigned simplicity, as the average man lacks the time to insightfully understand them all. The politicians themselves were like posters; a slogan was a sufficient form of description; everyone else did not need to know their depths of complexity in terms of personality and opinion. The simple man was likeable, the complex man was a miracle, but in many ways, a burden too.

I envied the powerful, ruthlessly analysed and tried to grasp the secrets of their elusive, but nonetheless, seemingly effortless hold on power. The seeds of their experience already persisted in childhood. I envied those with goodwill and who commanded the attention of everyone else with ease. They analysed, drew conclusions from what they saw and through their gently narrowed eyelids, their sneakiness was apparent. Was I just too intelligent to see what others saw? A cold manipulator putting on false appearances, their overall speech and demeanour not matching what they did? Maybe, it was me who was stupid, not seeing a goodwill, clouded by my burning envy and desire to obtain what they had.

I fed on the adulation of adults when I was younger. I had a sharp pang of pride whenever the teacher complimented, gave me an award, meaningless though it was, and made me feel happy as a result. However, there is always someone brighter than us, and the victor takes it all, and the rest are left with nothing. Tim joined the class, and yes, I was still good, but he had that extra edge. Every maths problem was solved quicker, and every thought expressed in a clearer way. I viewed him with a strange mix of resentment and admiration and had to make him my friend.

Every day I came back, and my father asked me how I was doing. He asked to see the number of gold stars that I had gotten and took it so very seriously. He produced graphs of my work and achievement and made sure that he documented everything that I did. I viewed as tyranny, but it was really an act of love gone wrong, all too terribly wrong. The pressure of intense scrutiny was dominating and made for a tense home environment.

The father could love us, but sometimes so passionately, that effort burnt out the natural spark of curiosity and cheerfulness that persisted in children.

17

She commanded attention and evoking desire. The eyes of the room fluttered quickly and turned to her. The gravitas and the tempo of the room increased, as the hearts of all those attendants pounded ever quicker with desire. I thought in images, and this was the image that I had always wanted to see in the world. The woman that everyone wanted to have was mine, and no one else could have her. I realised at that moment that I did not really love Laura, for someone as cold as me never knew what love felt like. I only wanted her, and the sheer desire that it would bring.

We argued all the time, and it was simply a case of me being spellbound.

She touched me on the shoulder, 'Just sit down and watch. Observe.'

'Why? This is a bit weird. Why do you want me to do this?'

'Not everything can be expressed in words. It is essential that you understand some things without recourse to language. This is about what you told me last Friday.'

'OK.' My abdomen tensed and I did not know what to say. I guess I would have to judge the message by the way that I felt at the end of what I saw.

Conversations between us got increasingly formal and businesslike.

The seat seemed like a theatre, and I achieved a dioramic view of proceeding, the drama augmented by the levels present and the variety of personages present. There was Laura, the innocent maiden, the meaty jocks and the slender runner, all in the aim of some elusive goals, health and beauty. The lighting was a certain tone to augment the form of the body, and the music was oddly motivational. I dreaded having to use the language of values as I believed it could not be related to the objective and therefore had no truth. Language, like any tool, had its limits.

Her hands were covered in chalk, and she dusted it off. Its misty precipitate created a fog and then floated to the floor. The limestone smell went into my nostrils, and I sneezed in irritation at the contents. She lifted the weights, and her legs and arms inflated. I was captivated. The weight rack shuddered at the increased mass of the system.

A huge breath of air was gulped in. Her chest inflated and was erect. I watched her breasts rub against her Lycra, and I was captivated. It took me a great effort to look away, so I did not embarrass myself. Lust was a natural part of the human condition, and I wanted to override it, but I could not. The desire for women was far too strong inside me.

The rhythm of the rising and falling weights lulled me into a dangerous kind of fascination.

Her arms contorted as she dropped the weights to the floor, and her skin was rosy with the fresh blood that had rushed into the surface.

Women were beautiful beyond all reasonable comparison. Since I was a child, I long imagined pressing myself against a body, feeling it, sensing it, becoming at one with it.

This is probably what love really felt like, the ocean effect, an altruistic morphing of the self into something greater. To a large extent, someone had to be everything in order to be loved. A personality defect was grossly undesirable, and when someone saw a bit of everything inside a person, it was difficult for them not to be loved. As we tend to know a person more and more, we tend to understand them, rationalise mistakes, and amplify their achievements in spite of the limitations that they have faced.

There were two ways of seeing the world: one, as characterised by mundane, rote processes, and the other were everything was a miracle of some sort. I tended to make things romantic, as such a view could only augment the beauty that the world possessed. Life was often ugly, and sometimes a rose-tinted view of the world was the only thing that could save us from insanity. Beauty was the effortlessness of action, as Immanuel Kant posited. I grew tired of trying to describe the language of values, for they never fitted the truth sufficiently enough. The good was only what we made of it.

I was sick of those prophets who said that they knew what good was and so what the bad was. A few years ago, I took part in a protest at a spiritual retreat for a sect. We shouted polite denunciations at the guru there and wanted a more rational, clear-minded view on the world. This power monger wound up these innocent people's brains into following a bastardised vision of the world. He lured them in with ambiguous statements but with a confidence that he was the remedy to all of their troubles. Leaders led via their charisma, not their reason.

The police came in and dragged us away into this cult leader's office. We were terrified, he thought that he was going to sacrifice us, humiliate us, do something dreadful, but the rest were OK. Except me, my fellow protesters were all led away, and it was just we in this ramshackle, wooden office. It was an hour of tensed silence as the policeman read out a cautionary warning and its implications for my life, which were, to say the truth, not enormous. I nodded and understood that I had messed up. The guru then wanted a chat, the officers went out the door, and no steps were heard. They were waiting right here.

'You are a fool, beyond all comparison. You think I am imposing my morals on these people? Well, you are doing just about the exact same thing!' He sighed in anger and rolled up his eyes. 'These people look for happiness, not for truth. After a certain level of spiritual understanding, you come to understand that there is no such thing as truth anyway.'

'No one is happy living a lie!' I shouted.

'Oh yeah, everyone lives a lie. There is no inherent meaning of life. You believe in this stupid idea of justice. Get out, you disgrace.' I ran past the sniggering officers.

18

After seeing that, I realised that I was a good man. I was prepared to face up to the few evils far and few between that my soul possessed. Reality was unusual, but I could stomach the truth. What was goodness? It seemed to be without a coherent answer, yet this question plagued me for the entirety of my short life. Was the good happiness, like Mill said? These things were far too difficult for a man to decide independently, and one had to choose, like the Grand Inquisitor in Dostoevsky's *The Brothers Karamazov*. I nodded and tried to hold back the tears clogging up my throat.

'See, I told you,' she gestured.

'Yeah, I guess it's normal to feel these things, especially for your girlfriend.'

'Yeah.'

'You're so beautiful when you do that.'

'That's why I do it. What's the point of all of this if it isn't beautiful?'

She was right; everything in our lives had to be good; otherwise, everything that we did could not be enjoyable.

We hugged. However, I still felt a growing gulf between us when I realised the differences in our identity. There was a clear reason why I liked Alice; she was closer to me in many ways than Laura was. Or so it seemed. I dreaded the long, arduous and necessary process that it took to know a person. It was either life beautifully or horribly spent.

Perhaps I just needed her validation. For so long, my parents chastised me, kept telling me persistently that I was somehow inadequate and not deserving of the things that I had. At first, I resisted, reacting with force to their claims and trying to shoo them away.

Humans, however, have an inherently cruel streak to them and they will persist in making you fluster and tired if you give them the opportunity to do so. One day, my force of character gave in, and I stopped believing in myself. So even though I was aware of this process, I never believed. It took a long time and many good people for me to believe in this once again.

I now had reason to believe that they envied me. For people strive to bring down those who are far above them. The bigger they are, the harder they fall, as the old adage goes.

People may not understand this, but this is often the case. So, we should stop trying to rationalise the flaws of others, changing ourselves to fit expectation and instead, just be as we are ourselves. We must fit in to survive, but no more. We should not be defined by the folly of those around us, and instead, be defined by our own. Happiness will not come from the approval of others, but instead, a stable sense of identity.

I used to want these things myself, but I dreaded the disapproval of others. Although I knew on a rational level that I was wrong to be doing certain things, the emotional pain that I felt whenever I was being subjected to some degree of criticism was acute, and I could scarcely persist and insist on my own point of view. Conversations with others became a pain, and it was difficult to go through them without some degree of disease.

Our beliefs were sure to restrict us at times, as had turned out for me, but changing them often proved to be a futile and pointless affair.

It hurt when I was rejected by people who I liked: prospective friends and lovers, who would not deign to say what they had found undesirable in me. At these times, I had felt alone, with little or no one out there to support me. These cases were tragic to an extent, but I bit my lip and continued on the trajectory that I had often set for myself. I was obsessed for months on end, even after the time had passed. The relationship that I had at the moment was able to heal all of that, but that woman's face will be imprinted on my mind forever.

It was then that I decided to change my life. No longer would I be someone who was persistently marginalised and made to feel inadequate. I decided to expel the fear that persisted inside me, and take responsibility for who I wanted to be. It was not that I feared harm, society tended to ensure sufficiently against that, but I needed to train out of me these dangerous pangs of self-consciousness and a sense of general anxiety. Only then could I start to cultivate a respect for myself. The desire to take conscious control of one's life is difficult and often necessitates an overbearing and overwhelming feeling of accountability.

The gym had a contemplation room, which I decided to use in search of an answer. There were times when the contents of my mind became too entangled, messy and a bit of a thing as a means of relaxation was the only way to calm the senses. I crossed my legs on the floor and laid out the mat.

I started to focus on the tips of my nostrils and felt pleasant shivering progressing up my spine. I tried to sit in silence and contemplate the darkness in my eyes. I got bored and got up.

I went to the common room and played snooker instead, for the boredom of what I had seen needed relief. Sure, what I was doing now was most definitely pointless, but the banal was what allowed sanity to occur in certain individuals like myself. The human mind needed to be crammed with content, for play and analysis to occur. A game was a brilliant moment of make believe to suspend oneself and immerse oneself in a brilliant game of enjoyment. How such a trivial affair could inspire such extreme emotions in humans shocked me. The whole room heard me when I potted the black ball.

Still, something was missing overall. I decided to go home and to relax. Light up a few candles, spend some time in front of the fireplace, just generally find a way to bring myself to a generally more relaxed mode of being. It was good to let the mind wander.

Attachment to things was dangerous, and like any animal, the mind needed to occasionally run free and not be committed to the tyranny of routine. When we rest, we end up performing better overall, though I had found it difficult to find the Middle Way, the feted optimal solution that was the secret to all the world's problems.

19

I return to the theme of dreams, something which is so dear to me that I am prepared to devote an excessively large amount of time to its discussion. My interest was provoked by some distressing childhood experiences with dreams, I had a repeated sensation that I was under attack, and my family was being hurt, and so, I needed to resolve these issues.

By controlling the unconscious recesses of my mind, these terrors which plagued me so often could finally be resolved, and I could begin to live a calmer life. A problem had to be tackled from its roots.

Taken away. Abandoned. Attacked. These were all primal childhood fears that played out in my brain, and I was not hurt by them because I understood the reason why such things occurred. So, I was not hurt by them. The monsters in our psyche, however, morphed into more complex versions of themselves, which proved to be terrifying. I had to learn to keep a leash on such things and interpret the world in a calmer manner. As children, we had our parents go, 'There, there' and pet us when things did not go according to plan. As adults, we had to internalise this instinct towards relaxation within ourselves.

I needed to be in control. People were safe when they knew what was going on and how to control the situation. As such, I held knowledge in the highest esteem, for the more we had, given the right emotional state, the more we could control the world around us. I obsessively studied in my youth to attain this positive state of mind. I kept shifting the perspective around me; sometimes hanging down from monkey bars, then lying down on the floor. Perspective was sometimes more important than substance. Higher states of consciousness were the goal.

I did a lot of reading about the topic on the Internet. I realised that there was a certain portfolio of techniques that could help me understand my dreaming even more. It mainly involved the hands. The idea was that I could look at my hands and judging by their state judge whether I was in reality or not. At first, in waking time, you check your hands every hour to see if they are still there. However, the mind naturally combats these activities of self-awareness by incorporating them into our dream states. So, I had to do something which involved a physical barrier. If I could put a finger through my hand, then it was a dream. If not, everything that I saw was a reality. This simple test is a good test for those who are versed in delusion and require external confirmation of the reality of our world.

I had a tendency to overanalyse and be sure of knowing certain things. I was not ready to accept something without adequate scrutiny and needed to always have a reason before I was ready to affirm something. Sometimes language fell apart, and anything that it proffered seemed to be an item of deceit, rather than truth.

'Are you sure?' I kept asking myself. I then saw that my decision-making was faltering as a result of such actions, and decided to resist the oppression of rationality that I had fostered upon myself. The academics had deemed too many heuristics as profane; it was the long odyssey of my adult life to claim them back again.

The Hindus said that everything was a dream at the end of the day, with Creation being something that unfolded from the mind of God in his sleep. This idea of dreams is quite prominent in many indigenous cultures. When he woke, Creation would be destroyed, and the world would go into a phase of non-existence. We should put less emphasis on the present moment, and accept the fact that some parts of our life are close to irrelevant, due to their triviality and impermanence. There was a little point being attached to material possessions, due to their conditionality and impermanence. Though there was no way of definitively proving such a view, we sometimes had to accept a certain view to defend our reality.

Still, I did not want to lie to myself. There was a burning desire for authenticity in my soul and strongly desired to live a life true to myself and wanted to be free of empty convention, others' opinion, form for its own sake, rather than substance in itself. I remembered the words of Sartre, saying that one had to choose for himself, and nobody else in order to preserve the authenticity that they possessed. This was another absolute value that was clothed in the complexity of Man, and this great thinker had done us the service of discovering it.

What we believed was fundamentally real: that was a dizzying realisation to find and somehow accept. I wanted to make sure that other people would also accept such a tenet. It is something that we all know, in reality, inside us, but it is difficult to articulate to the outside world, which would deem us pig-headed and frankly, blind. I did not know why

I contemplated these things, but my mind pushed me in a direction where I only asked questions and could not find an answer. I felt aroused by the excitement of spirituality; perhaps that was the reason for my contemplation.

I wanted to have access to another dimension of reality as a means of attaining self-knowledge and refining and reforming my beliefs even further.

I was glad that I was honest with myself. I was content that I could be honest with myself like that. And control my reality better.

Laura licked her lips and proceeded towards me; something strange was going on. I may have provoked some kind of arousal. The passion I felt was too strong. I could not though. I grasped Laura's hand and then I walked off with her.

'We shouldn't do that,' I said. She smiled, gently nodding.

20

I knew that there were certain dreams that had a repeated occurrence in my mind, and they tended to be of the most absurd nature. That was the good option because the other was immersion into something totally terrifying. Dreams of kidnappings, discomfort, injuries, were so common, but yet so unfounded that it was hard not to think of these as prophecies for the future of some sort. Our bodies must have been evolutionarily wired for these kinds of shocks, so it was no great surprise to see them. We should not judge against pessimism; it is an integral part of the human condition.

I sat on my quilt and rubbed my eyes. Before me, Descartes had appeared.

'Hello, I think we have met before.' My vision was slightly blurry from all the rubbing, but I then my vision seems normal.

'Yes, I think we have.' I walked to the door and tried to put my finger through my hand.

Nothing happened, and I checked that reality did not radically change around me. This was no dream; a madman dressed as a philosopher was sitting in my room. I covered the door but did not lock in case I had to flee.

'Reveal yourself, or I'm calling the police.' I slid my hand into my pockets to show I was being serious. I had to spread my body to stop him from running out of the door. He let out a large sigh and moved out his neck forward. My eyes lit up in terror, and my focus was completely directed towards this intruder.

He put his hand on his chin and then stroked it. 'In that case, I'm going out through the window. Don't worry; I'm prepared. I've got a rope.'

'What? Don't you dare.'

He calmly stepped towards the window and started opening the pane.

'You'll kill yourself!' I screamed. Outside got brighter as curious onlookers must have turned on their lights.

I was not sure if this individual was about to die deliberately or accidentally, but I had to put a stop to it.

Silence. It was chilling. He stood still for thirty seconds, and I realised that I had to act. He was preparing something, a line of some sorts. He looked to be tying it to the railings with some complex knot.

I knew I had to act. Either way, this could end very badly.

I ran hard and barged him in this hip with my shoulder. Something grated inside me, but I persisted, the adrenaline numbing the pain that will have emerged. He shrieked, and was on the ground, his face reddening up. He was clothed in thick fabric to seem a man, and to shield him against the frigid cold air. He was weak, a young boy lacking masculine strength, but nonetheless, willing to survive and he clung on, desperately, to the radiator's tubes, afraid that I would rip him apart. Beyond his prosthetic mask, his face quivered, and I felt the lack of character that only children would have. I felt the rage in my muscles and realised that I had a Beast inside me as well. Evil and goodness existed in every human being, and my evil side was open right there. Courage was a very elusive thing in many people, and it disappeared or spontaneously emerged, depending on the situation. This figure seemed familiar, and a part of me wanted to cuddle up next to him. I was the Roaring Lion, a figure of courage, even if I did look rather ridiculous. Still, the most courageous sometimes look like fools. Winston Churchill was a national hero after all, and look where he came from.

I had to calm down, but I could not let this figure slip away. He had to be punished for being in my room before and today. It had to stop now, or this maniac could come again, and maybe even hurt me one day. Evil had to be crushed in its fledgling steps, or it could sprout up to become an atrocity.

'It was you a month ago, wasn't it?' I enquired. The boy wheezed out and coughed. The pitch of his voice changed into a higher tone. He panted deeply, his hands becoming twitchy.

'Yes, it was me.' An uncomfortable silence lasted several seconds.

'Please get off me!' He shrieked.

Part of me knew that I needed to hold this abnormal person down. He was getting emotional and could be dangerous. I was running out of energy and needed some sort of a break, so I could gather my forces back. I empathised with this strange figure and decided to stop hurting him. The impulses of the human mind were very contradictory, and it was possible to feel both violence and empathy at moments in time very close to one another.

I got up, straightened my clothes and decided to pick up the phone.

'Stay down now!' I shouted at the figure, and he willingly obeyed, muttering a hum of approval, too tired to move. Now, either this person is pretending, or he is unusually weak, and he reminded me of my sickly brother, who had daring, but was too weak and immediately withered away from any sense of confrontation. That is how our father managed to lord it over us. I felt sorry for the young lad and had not seen him in the space of over a year. Nevertheless, I could not let empathy get in the way of my safety. I dialled 999 on the phone and worried that I could get myself into a pickle over a minor misunderstanding.

I looked at the ceiling and chose my words carefully. I did not know if I had injured this sickling, and I did not want him to press charges against me too.

The boy raised his head up, and I heard the sound of snivelling. He was crying.

I had to speak now.

'You better take off that mask right now, or you could be in serious trouble for intruding on me,' I urged the lad.

He took the mask off, and I saw his face. I let out a silent scream.

21

'What the hell are you doing here?' I shouted. 'It's midnight, and you're two hundred miles away from home! You've got a lot of explaining to do, mate.'

He threw away the costume on the floor and was dressed in normal clothes. His face was red, and a thin layer of sweat covered his skin, and he needed water fast. I came over to the tap and poured out a glass of water for him. He wolfed it down fast, and his hyperventilation reduced until he was breathing at a normal pace. I patted him on the back and stroked him. I could scarcely believe that a moment ago I was fighting my own brother, and it brought back fond memories of when I was doing so a decade ago. Even the negative aspects of our lives had positive elements.

'You have a lot of explaining to do.'

The door knocked. It was opened by the porter, eager to understand what was going on inside.

'Is everything all right?' she looked confused by the scene of my brother lying down on the floor. I shook my hands and convinced that nothing untoward had happened.

'Don't worry, ma'am. He's had a busy night out, and he feels exhausted. That's all.'

'Well, if there's anything that I can help with, please ask!' She gently rolled her eyes and exited the room. I was happy that I did not lie to her, but I quickly phrased myself in the right way. Deceit, under my code, was acceptable, as it was on the listener to interpret correctly. Saying an outright lie, misrepresenting the truth was not, as the proposition uttered gives no way of understanding the truth.

'Why did you want to climb out of the window? What were you thinking?' I asked.

'I was gonna climb out via the rope.' I looked inside his rucksack and found some kind of a harness in there. Derek was a weirdo, even more so than me, but he had some sort of plan worked out. The irrationality of Mankind was enlightening, how Derek was even less afraid of falling to his death potentially in an abseiling catastrophe, then meeting his very own brother. Some dark things happened to us when we were with each other at home, and I did not quite understand why he would not want to speak to me. I did not do anything exceptionally wrong to him, aside from typical brotherly conflict. The little fights, the gentle teasing. It was reciprocal, and to be honest, I was the only ally he had in the house.

'Why didn't you call me? Why did you dress up as a dead philosopher to talk to me and convince me I was in a dream?'

He simply replied, 'I wanted to see you.'

'You know, because of you, I felt like I've been going mad for ages. I wasn't sure whether that was real before, but the world seems too ordered to be in an actual dream. Why didn't you just call, like others do?'

I had learnt the art of choosing words carefully to convey the same meaning, without offending the person that I was conversing with.

'I was embarrassed of myself. So, I put on this costume to mask who I really was. Look at me, I look pathetic.'

I growled in anger. 'There are only two things pathetic about you, Derek: your attitude and the fact you do elaborate things like this at the expense of the simple.'

'It's not simple for me. You know, confronting people.'

'Then become educated in it. Some people are geniuses in it, that's OK. There are others who have to persist day in and day out in obtaining what they want. That's what you have to do.'

'It's hard.'

'I know it is, but you'll either mess up your opportunities, or other people will take advantage of you. It's plain and simple.' His eyes filled up with tears and his lip was quivering.

'Look, did you come here for my sympathy? Yes, the house is tough, father is brutal, but we have it well. We had a roof over our heads, plenty of toys to play with and despite all their flaws, our parents really do love us. You do need help, though, what you did was quite worrying.'

'They'll ground me!'

'And rightly so! You've been acting very dangerously today. Do Mum and Dad even know you've come this far?'

'All they know is that I've gone to the supermarket.' He smirked. 'You're starting to sound like Mum and Dad now.'

'I have too. They probably fell asleep while you travelled by train here?'

'Wrong, I took the car.'

'You're too young to drive.'

'Wrong, Gabe, I'm already seventeen.' He frowned and looked to the side. 'And you forgot my birthday.'

'You're right; I just got carried away with the new life I had here. It's like everything here is so much better then back in Southport, and you kind of just want to stay in the good life here and forget the past.'

'You're my brother. The only one I have.'

'You're right. I should have reminded myself. Family is important, and we've probably got to protect them over our own happiness.'

We sat facing each other and looked around. Derek was analysing my room and looking at the writings on the wall. His nose twitched up, betraying an attitude of disdain. Being apart and spending time in different places makes you drift apart, I guess.

'You've changed.'

'I know.'

He heaved a breath out and asked, 'Is this really who you want to be? These snoots who deceive everyone and are responsible for life in our town? This isn't really you, and if it is, I am ashamed to be your brother. You even speak differently.'

I thought about how I would explain myself, and he was right. Throughout my teenage years, I had rubbished the elite, moralising against them, saying they did wrong to us. On a deeper level, I knew I was just jealous, and as soon as I joined them, I gladly played along.

How could I express such a thing, without losing Derek's respect?

'We can't change the system; we have to make our lives better.'

Derek shook his head. 'You can.'

22

The suffering was over. Finally, the years of hard work paid off. Or so it seemed. I saw classmates who worked for less and sometimes got even more from me. I was successful, but I knew that I had not lived up to my potential. And that seemed like a disappointment to me. I was a perfectionist, so I knew that I had to triumph in almost everything that you did. They said that you can't have everything; that's not true, but it is only a privilege limited to the very few. I knew that I was doing something wrong in my life and it was my duty to change it.

I resolved to be more conscious in my decision making. Every thought about what I had to do had to be documented as a logical argument. I decided to keep my thinking flexible, conservative in my method, but liberal in the particular pathways that I took. I asked myself questions all the time, and I was determined to make a change to what I was doing. Consciousness was a gift from God, and I was determined to exploit it to its fullest.

I engaged in activities like meditation and prayer, as a means to improve my self-consciousness. Knowledge was always good; that was the mantra I kept telling myself.

We got to sit on the tables at the graduation ceremony with our friends. There was me and Laura, Jed and Kayla and Toby and Ruby. We were not part of a big group, but we were a happy little collective, and we enjoyed good quality time together. I was a large round table, and I picked out the best seat in the house as always, facing the stage and in full view of it. I did not have to manoeuvre around my chair; I was calm and in control. That is until I saw the person who was speaking then.

I looked at Laura in her beautiful dress and I was absolutely infatuated with her. She possessed a tight, loose-lipped charisma and her bulging breasts were highlighted by the thin padding of the chest area of her dress. Her sweat emitted alluring pheromones and we somehow felt both animals again. But a small void formed inside me. There was a growing distance between us; we liked each other on a sexual level, but really, we started to have a growing disparity between us. We seemed incompatible with each other; I don't really know why we were still together. Habit was the answer, I guess.

'It's been three years together, huh?' I asked her.

'Yeah, it's been a long time…' she replied.

'You know, I feel like we're not moving on in any way.'

'What do you mean?'

'Well, we hang out with each other, have nice chats, but it just feels like it's not enough.

You know.'

'Is this because we don't have sex?' she asked.

'Ummm, yeah…' her eyes fluttered away, and she stood up and walked away. Thank God we were alone at that moment; the whole conversation was an embarrassment.

I wish that I could have been more refined in the way that I spoke to others; it led to catastrophes like these.

The sommelier came up to the table and started pouring out the wine.

'Do your companions require wine, sir?' the waiter enquired.

'I would assume that they do; no one has refused to have wine.'

I thought about my actions and recognised the need to persistently reflect upon them.

The red liquid oozed out of the bottle and swirled around the glass gently becoming its form. The smell of currants and antioxidants slowly filled my nose, and I started gently swaying from side to side, going into what seemed a rather blissful sleep. I was awoken by the sound of friends returning to the table.

'Grub's up, eh,' Toby shouted.

'Yeah, the best of the best,' I replied. Everyone sat down, and we had a lot to try out. They brought out an artisanal spaghetti Bolognese, encrusted with delicious wafers of parmesan cheese.

I looked out of place with my fish dish, but I did not care: I decided to eat anyway. I put the napkin onto my thighs and then resolved to tuck in. I found the formality strangely comforting, and revelled the role of being enforced into something that was not too oppressing, but actually something rather delightful. Freedom was overrated and could carry more responsibilities than was adequately appropriate. I understood what Orwell meant in Nineteen Eighty-Four when he declared freedom as slavery. Being free in the usual sense could result in us becoming slaves to our passions and to the slavery of responsibility in our decision-making.

The dean of the university was up to make a speech, and there was no secret of her willingness to flaunt her grandiosity in front of us. She was a scientist, meaning they claimed to know everything, but their myopia and bizarre commitment to the idea of reason blinded them. These nerds blinded themselves with their science; it was only marginally better than the devotionalism of organised religion.

Bergen said, 'Young people, above all, believe in your reason, and everything else should be subordinate to the noble quest for truth. Think with your minds, and not with your hearts.' Nonsense.

I was enraged and tired of the world, thinking differently to me. For all my life, people had kept telling me that I was wrong and I continued to vehemently disagree with them. I resented the capacity for harm that other people and for some reason, had a very high reactivity to words. It was a mystery that bewitched me for a long time.

'Thank God this lady is going to retire, pfft…' I blurted out, and my friends were visibly shocked. That could have just been the alcohol, but in alcohol, there is truth. Silence reigned the table, and it was clear that I had said something inappropriate in quite a formal setting.

Jed replied, 'I don't know, I think what she said kind of made sense. We should sort of be sceptical about what we believe, not always be emotional.'

I sensed that there was some kind of a personal attack embedded in the comment, and my face flushed, anger came to my face and my lip twitched with agitation. Socialising was all about maintaining appearances, and it was essential that I did not seem too angry, but my displeasure clearly did show.

I let out an internalised sigh and said, 'I guess each to their own,' and it was clear to me that such controversial topics ought not to even be discussed with friends. Sometimes you could only tell the truth to your friends.

23

I walked outside across the courtyard and fields nearby. I knew that I would find her in her favourite place, and I really knew that she was not hiding from me. This was all part of some elaborate game to trap me, a game of cat & mouse, in order to get something out of me. She did these things, acquiring a collection of goods and clothing that I had bought from her out of pity and forgiveness, although she definitely had more money than me to pay for such things. I never understood this distance between us, and somehow it had grown more clear and pronounced over the last few months. I notice other couples; how they would act normally, hang ties on their doors every once in a while. This was not the case for ourselves.

Laura: **He paced towards me, and he looked enraged. Eyes flaring up with blood and sadness, for he was a creature of real power. He was alluring, a man who had plenty of spirit, but was terrifying at moments like this as well. That was really why I had stayed away. I loved him, to the point of a cult, but I feared being crushed. That was what others told me, humiliated, but somehow empowered. I did not things I could cope with a maelstrom**

of such new feelings in such a short space of time. There was a reason that he was so quiet most of the time. He was aware of the fact that his true nature could push so many over the brink.

'So, you here again?' I asked.

'Yep.'

'You better come back; they're handing out the degrees soon.'

She looked at my face coldly, with her eyes piercing my own. 'I've already got mine.'

'Well, you should see me getting mine then!'

A little tear rolled down her face, and she wiped it away. She sighed, and shook her hand in my direction, ushering me off.

'What did I say?' the sound of silence was the only thing that greeted me.

I thought about how I was behaving from the side. I was confrontational; I had entered her sanctuary. In other words, a grave social sin was being committed, and I looked angry and terse as well.

'You know what your problem is Gabe. You think the world revolves around you and everything you do is somehow connected to yourself. You never take the time to think about other people, and when you do, it is only for your own gain. The procedure with which you offer altruism is so regimented, such as to render it false, and your actions irrelevant.'

'Have you had a little too much to drink, dear?' I chuckled along and realised how pretentious I sounded when I uttered that vocative.

'This is why you don't really have any friends, Gabe. I mean, why are you here? They upset you, or you upset them, something went on. I have enough reason left even when I am left in this state to say this much. You are a loner. That is why you spend so much time in your books and thinking.' I pursed my lips and tried to understand what she had said. The truth was searingly painful, and I hated Laura for it. It would not have hurt if it were not true.

However, I respected her for saying such a statement, admiring her for her candour, whereas others will have just uttered half-truths or layers of deceit.

I wasn't that weak, however.

'Why do you like me, then?'

'You look like my dad.'

'Excuse me?'

'I'm kidding, although it's true.'

'Right.' I got what she was saying, and relaxed, getting the reference. Sigmund spoke.

'That's the real reason; we smart people know that. But what I feel is different.'

'Different?'

'I look and see a fragile soul. Someone misunderstood perhaps. Lost in a superficial world. A person of great kindness.'

'And someone who looks incredible as well.'

'Yes, that too,' she grudgingly nodded.

'Someone of value in this homogenous world.'

'Love has to wait sometimes, doesn't it?'

'It does. Only scarce things are valuable, and must earn them from each other.'

I nodded and played with my fingernails, theorising about what I would proffer to Laura next. I breathed a sigh of relief, having avoided a potential catastrophe. But desire welled up in my heart, and I could not restrain myself from what I was about to say next.

'You know, a lot of this seems unfair though.'

'Unfair, how?'

'You know, I do a lot for you.'

'Yeah, and I for you. What are you getting at?'

'It's just; I buy these things, and…'

'Yeah?'

'You have these nice handbags and designer clothes and…'

'What?' There was power in cutting someone off at a volta, letting domination proceed to the interrupter.

'Well, what have I got from you?'

'Excuse me?'

'I mean we have really great fun together, but honestly, sometimes; I just don't feel your love.'

'You don't?'

'You know, my family are having it hard with the finances, and I just buy all these things for you.'

'Well, then don't buy them.'

'I feel like I have to?'

'No, you don't. Like I don't.'

'Sorry?'

'If you think all of this is just based on paying for each other's lives, then I don't want a single bit of it.' She told me to go away, and I obeyed.

I thought about what Laura had said, and it was clear that I was behaving selfishly, and did not really understand what people needed. It was wrong of me to ever bring material things into the equation. Although her lust for items did not mean that she did not love me, it was wrong for me to cloud the material with the spiritual. Love was a feeling, a positive state of mind, and it confused people, even her, as to why someone was really loved.

Was it because of the goods I offered or my personality? These were difficult questions to ponder, maybe pointless at the end of the day. I tried to remove them from my mind as I went to collect my degree, and offered a smile of pain, though my mind kept returning to the mistakes of the minutes before.

24

I found out the truth, but not from her directly. I was shocked by how our loved ones often did not dare to speak the truth to us, perhaps because of a fear of hurting us. I found out from our buddies that Laura had decided to consider a move to America. Of course, she did not tell me because I would be left all alone and that would surely deliver her guilt. I was alone and what I needed was company. I understood that love was a relationship of equals, and that precipitated respect for one another, although it was still paramount that the rights of the individual were respected in such a case.

But I was greedy, selfish beyond reasonable belief, and I did not want to lose such a precious asset, so I considered my plan beyond the immediate period ahead. Was I to stop her or to let her fly? In matters of the heart, there were no logical or mathematical answers, and it riled me. I had to know that I was doing the right thing, and I found out that my experience was tantamount to abandonment. I had to wait until the right moment and then strike once I had discovered the solution to this troubling conundrum. I needed to be aware of what I could possibly do next.

I decided to lie in wait outside the embassy. The building was covered in a portfolio of sophisticated tessellations, and its box-like nature concealed the prominence that it sported relative to the surroundings it possessed. It was a hub of power, no doubt, demonstrated by its alternative style architecture and premium position next to the river, but was not overly exotic. For power must be somehow maintained by modesty, such that it is inspiring to its followers and such that the acid of envy does not erode the stability that such a system has. The foyer looked polished, presentable, and was standard of a state with plenty of money, one that could make the bureaucratic procedure look elegant at will.

The wanderlust that many people possessed was inexplicable, but I posited that such an idea was hypocritical, given that I too had decided to venture out into the world beyond my immediate sphere, and I was not totally clear whether this was exactly something to regret. My town was dingy, a constructivist relic in a post-industrial wasteland, but I loved the area nonetheless. It was the place of my forefathers, thousands of years into the past, and I dearly loved every single person who walked through those streets. Even my enemies, years later, I bear them no grudges, simply because I knew they were my family to some extent. Blood is thicker than any other liquid on Earth.

I kept telling myself that my leave was only temporary. I was one of those people who left their homeland to study and promised myself that I would return after I had finished. But my three years were up, and I had made no plans to return. Rather, I was still in Cookton, renting my student accommodation, wondering as to what my next plans would end up being. I was probably lying to myself, and I did not want to go back to the way that I was.

The world was an intensely rewarding place, and the sinews of ambition forever spurred me onto the unknown.

Love had made me stagnate, forget about the world around me and about the future. It was a joyous living in the moment. They said that happiness found its base there. Oh, I was not so sure anymore. One was in bliss in the moment, but without preparing, protecting oneself from the unknown, one's life could quickly descend into an intense form of despair. One had to review the past, but still hedge oneself from the effects of the future. In a pair, I had gradually drifted further from my friends, Jack in particular.

Therefore, I was delighted when the phone rang, and I glanced and saw his name on the screen below.

As the skyscrapers of London wafted pass me as the cabdriver drove me, I was delighted to hear from my old friend after a couple of months.

'Jack, how are you? We are so close, yet seemingly so far!'

He laughed quietly in the background.

'That's one way of putting it.'

'How have you been then?'

'I've been all right and would like some advice. But first, tell me about yourself.'

'Just graduated last week, and now I don't know what to do?'

'Have you found a job?'

'I'm currently not sure about what I want to do. Laura might want to move abroad, so I have to plan around that.'

'Right.'

The conversation stagnated, and I wanted to lift the heavy weight of conversation off my shoulders.

'So what do you want to know about then?'

'It's about my work.'

'Your work?'

'Yeah, my boss is an absolute psychopath and he absolutely humiliated me.'

'What did he do?'

'He threw a banana skin at me in a fit of rage.'

My mouth opened in disgust when I heard what this superior had done to my friend. It was absolutely horrible to hear of one's friends being treated horribly like that.

'So what are you going to do then?'

'The way I see it is there are three options: you get the bastard dismissed, leave the Service or transfer to another department.'

'I don't want to leave. I love what I do; just I hate him so much.'

'Then complain.'

'He's terrified the office into submission and controls all the tapes. Everything goes through him.'

'He's taken away your honour – what's the worst that can happen?'

'I'll be fired from the Service, and it will be ten years of work undone.'

'Go about it intelligently then. Sometimes conflict is unavoidable.'

In that moment, I felt like the voice of evil. However, sometimes, evil is unavoidable if we are to survive. War was the right thing for Jack, although it was horrible, and no other reasonable alternative was in sight for him.

25

A common theme that we encounter as children is whether fate exists as a phenomenon.

It is a theme countlessly repeated in the literature we see, and the myth that we are often fed is that the world is within our hands, everything is within our control, for they believe that the world is both free and fair. But as we approach adulthood, we are humbled into see our limitations as humans, both for good and for ill, and we see ourselves as fragile boats, tossed around the seas of life by the weather, and the captains of our souls have a limited effect.

I looked back on the events of my life often and contemplated how I could have done better. Of course, I was happy, without a doubt, I had all the things requisite for a good human life, but I was never content. I was dissatisfied with the acts of folly that I had often committed, for nothing was enough. I had the heart of a pig. Nothing more hurt than having another human being prove their superiority over me on my terms, especially when they did so with contempt, leaving me unknowing and unable to act and strike back.

Powerlessness was a horrible feeling.

I needed to decide what to do with my life and how to interpret Laura's signals. Was this a desire to flee me or a society that had become foreign to me? I knew over the past year, I had become more skilled in reading people's intentions and signals, but they still seemed a black box to me. I think on a fundamental level, I did not really care, for other people often seemed like too much of a burden to me. And an attempt to understand them was not really worthwhile. There was no real right answer to my question, but there was surely one that felt right.

Days passed where there were no thoughts in my head. I tried to grapple with ideas, with numbers, with issues, but the mind lacked the will. Things like happiness and willpower were not permanent states of mind or character, for every human being was in flux. Rather they were reserves, to be replenished and eroded by the events that happened in our environment. I went to the café and stared outside the window, trying to make sense of how I got to such a point of uncertainty. I simultaneously regretted that I had not been more mindful and conscious of what I had done before, juxtaposed with a sense of satisfaction that persisted due to the relaxation and blissful ignorance that I had before.

But a moment was a point, something with no dimension, so the only thing that really mattered was how I felt at this point in time. Adulthood was a time of life, for many, characterised by an exhilarating confusion, which coincided in a miraculous or disastrous alignment of circumstances. Wisdom was needed, and it could not be taught or systemically learned, only unveiled through a prodigious mind or years of arduous experience. Wise men were not a thing of the past, and it was great to bump into one once in a while.

I felt a tap on my shoulder, and I turned around. It was Jansen, and I should have expected to see him.

'Gabriel, how are you doing?' he stretched out his hand and shook mine.

'I'm OK, don't know about the future though.'

He smiled, 'It seems like you need someone to talk to. Come buy me a drink – you're not under my authority anymore.'

'OK.'

'What are your plans after the summer?'

'You see, I'm not so sure.'

'You're not sure? You've been here for three years – there must be some kind of an idea.'

'No, I'm still stuck.'

'OK, do you know what you want to do? What is your passion?'

'I want to write.'

'That is an honourable calling. Now, what do you feel obliged to do?'

'My parents say I should work harder. Study more.'

'Why do they say these things?'

'They say work hard and have a happy life. I tell you, hard work never got me to a good place.'

'Were you always a professor?'

'Of course not. I went down the route that everyone else went down; it was the rat race. It was a time of incessant work, the days stretched out into a long period of labour, and I started to forget who I was outside of my job. I felt like every day was a battle was one against myself and one of constant self-abnegation. Corporations took my soul out of me, and I decided to follow my passion, teaching.'

'Well, sir, the thing is that I like working in these companies. I mean they're so attractive, and I like the work. I find it something quite effortless and enjoyable. It's my art form, making these documents, talking to these rich people. I love the corporate life, but I want to be an entrepreneur. Create value.'

'Sounds boring,' he nodded and laughed.

He sighed. 'On a serious note, though, you do seem quite sure of yourself in terms of your job. You seem to be unhappy with something else. You're beating around the bush.'

'It's more to do with where I live, I guess. My girlfriend wants to move to America?'

'Oh, OK.'

'Yeah, she's hungry for opportunities.'

'And you're not so sure?'

'Yeah, exactly.'

'Do you love her?'

'I don't know. And I'm starting to doubt myself more and more.'

'What is love to you?'

'It's a longing to be with someone, that is without violation.'

'So?'

'I don't know if I want to be with her, I don't know if I really want to be with anyone. I find myself happy alone, and with the world at my feet.'

'Do you have any friends?'

'I have had friends before, but I constantly find myself drifting apart. People never stay the same.'

'Go for the effortless path.'

I looked outside the window, and he was gone.

26

Laura sent me a message and said that she wanted to meet opposite the US Embassy.

She knew that I knew and it was clear that we had to get things straight. It was a warm summer's day, and the park was the only place we could speak. People complained of being bereft of privacy in the modern age, but the way that our institutions secretly oppress the privacy we so praise. The university rooms' walls were paper thin, we (rightly) lived in groups called families, but the rules that societies required and the fears that other members inspired within us prevented us from fully expressing ourselves.

The park was vast and boundless, and there would be a corner in which to have an honest conversation and in close proximity, in front of the world, but away from people who could judge. We met outside the embassy and then had a chat about our week. Even when you know someone, small talk eases the difficulty of conversation, and it becomes simple to conduct oneself.

'How have you been?' I asked.

'OK.'

For a minute, only the sound of the road and the bumbling footsteps of the pedestrians.

'So, why didn't you tell me? What did I do wrong?'

'I cannot explain these things now; let's take a seat on a bench.'

And so we did. Luckily the trees soon began, and I made sure that we faced inland and not towards the river. Water was a chance to immerse oneself in the unknown, connect to a greater reality. And of course, it would make us emotional.

'So, let's talk.'

'I didn't want you to stop me.' At this point, a huge surge of negativity opened up inside me, and the taste of metal returned to my mouth.

'How could I? You already did.' I was not sarcastic, but showed no emotion: my heart grew hard from these encounters.

'You'd talk me out of it. Say, America is not for me.'

I knew that every word in such a case would matter, but I was tired of thinking what to say next. Most of what was said and done by me I had realised had no impact on the world whatsoever and admiring oneself in conflict was the most sure way of being sunk by it. I surrendered myself to my feelings and just was. Thinking was a burden, and it seemed right that I could just be.

I spoke the truth and contemplated the sheer lies that had sometimes left my mouth. It was lies, all lies, and every bit of flattery and evasion slowly wore away the soul. Even deception and misleading, distorting the truth to fit my purposes became sickening, and I was fed up of clothing myself to please and appease. I knew that the only way one could pretend to be another was through humour, sheer humour, which was never really a becoming one with the object of our desire. Humour, in many ways was a mockery, and the only way to defend oneself from it was a way to defeat their opponent. Words and ideas had to be minimised, as they collapsed into a quagmire of self-doubt, and I wanted to say as little as I could.

I remembered the film *A Thousand Words* and wanted to be liberated from the urging of others for me to speak. They said words could change the world and were the foundation of our freedom, but I believed that they left us increasingly trapped in dogma. Logic could not help either: it was just a set of connections between words. I felt the world zooming out and then zooming back in, such that reality had become destabilised.

'I understand that you would be upset.'

My soul went back into my body, and I did not know whether what I had experienced was good or not, but I felt like days had passed when the watch said it was a single moment.

I had started to believe in the power of intense experience and what it really told us.

'I don't know what to say. Do you not trust me or something?'

'No, I just feel…increasingly distant from you.'

'Distant? After all, I have given you? Are you not making yourself even more distant from me by going away – without even telling me?'

I understood why I had often stood silent when injustices were committed, and I was treated unfairly. My emotions were never strong, and the drive to conformity was the thing that persisted. My brain was wired to do the right thing, and only these restrictions could be transcended by the feeling of rage. Good, nor evil was really a choice, but merely a way of programming, and I felt blessed with my peace, but sometimes disliked the inbuilt leash that it kept with me.

'I had put so much love into this. And yet I waited. I could have drowned myself in sex, in pure pleasure during the best years of my life. But I loved you. I don't know why, but I just did. I don't know if you did.'

'What do you mean, of course, I do!' I mistrusted her intensely.

'Really, and you only tell me now!' Sarcasm seeped through the gaps of my teeth. The frozen sea in my soul was broken by something, and I felt conscious of everything. The blood pouring through every capillary, each alveolus animated by the oxygen of life, the birth of every thought in my head. Although one thing I was not sure of: was this folly, pure emotional stupidity or the truth, finally unmasked in a flurry of explosions?

I was not calm for sure, I was neurotic, and I was tired of masking these sentiments towards the world.

'Are you breaking up with me?' Tears gathered in her eyes, and her face became crimson, augmented by the warm glow of the sun outside.

I was emotive, but I had never stopped feeling what I really did. I did not want to choose, but I knew I had to.

'I don't know anymore,' I replied. 'You moving away, it's kind of hard to maintain a relationship on that distance.'

I knew that on that park bench, I was faced with a choice that would determine the rest of my life. I realised that I reasoned through this moment a million times before already and my heart did not give me a coherent answer either. I tried to suspend thought and listened to the sensations that I had felt around me. A mass of pressure built up at the bottom of my stomach and my thoughts were stopping me from saying the forbidden words, but I had to relax and release the tension. I often stopped myself from living the life that I truly wanted, and courage was a hard thing to attain.

'Well, I know what you're going to say, you coward,' she said so with disdain and with a calm tone of voice, accepting her fate. Only then could I continue.

'I think we'll have to call it a day,' I offered.

She nodded and proffered a smile of disappointment. 'I see.'

'It looks like you don't mind yourself.'

'Yeah, I guess.'

We conducted ourselves calmly and civilly, just like friends. It was great to see that there was no real drama and that we had not exploded into negativity.

Only then, once our intentions were clear, could the real conversation begin.

27

She was about to smile and leave.

'Can I explain myself?' I offered.

'I feel that we are not ready for each other, there's kind of uncertainty in what we do, and I know that a relationship far away cannot really work. Also, I love the place I live in so much; I don't dare think of leaving. UK is not perfect, but neither is America. I'd rather be in a place where I'm welcome, where I'm not.'

'Come on, America is a very welcoming place. There's a lot of immigrants there.'

'In law, of course, that's true. But unless you become someone who you're not, and I have no intention of renouncing who I am, then I would rather stay where I am.'

'You're arrogant, that's what.'

'Perhaps, but that still does not mean that I want to renounce my identity at the end of the day. I do not want to be a chameleon, shifting from place to place, and would rather be part of a fixed place, and maybe with my family.'

'What about finding yourself; collecting experiences?'

'Maybe you need to do it, but I'm boring. I think this thing is dangerous and leads to a life where nothing is certain, and you keep moving around. You need a connection to something, and that, to have any meaning, has to be held in a fixed place.'

'You've changed.'

'We all do.'

She got up and offered to walk back to the station.

'You know why I liked you?'

'Why?'

'Because you're smart.'

'Why don't you like me anymore?'

'You've become too boring.'

'I guess boredom's just being too smart.'

'You know, it's more than that. You love these boring careers; you just want to sit at home, before you know it you'll be stuck in a dead-end job for the rest of your life.'

'I love what I do, though. That's the key. All these sales and accounts are a great way to pass one's time.'

'I guess we had an affection, compatible personalities, but we have no common interests.'

'The third missing pillar of any successful relationship.'

We both laughed along.

'Who knows that changes. We don't know what the future holds?'

'I've got to go another way, but before you leave, I want to say two things. Let's meet if we see each other somewhere else and thank you for teaching me humour. It's a great tool.'

'Don't worry. I'm glad I've made you slightly less robotic.' I did a little jiggety jig.

I guess what I learnt that time with her was that life was some kind of a journey and it consisted of being happy at where you were at the moment, and I was not sure with her.

The prize always seems like an oasis from afar, but you can often stumble onto a block of desert land and suffer for years.

Laura was a good person, but was either not the right time or the right person for me.

My father taught me that if something felt wrong, and for all his strange tendencies, it was right. The right thing is something immediately apparent, and we must transcend the fear that we face to accomplish it. I had the courage to speak through doing nothing.

I learnt to stop being swayed by social pressures more, the pressure to have a wife, a girlfriend, any form of a partner. I had to take responsibility for my own life and decide to live independently myself. Sometimes we must stand alone, even if not forever. Being one gave you the right to choose, and that did not mean being alone! We were just more free to choose who we wanted to be with.

I did pine and reflect for a bit and looked at the photos of the good times we had together. Rowing on the lake, feeding the ducks, overall, the good times with our friends. I flicked through and for the first time in a long while cried a bit. Tears represented sadness, sure: but the saddest times in my life were when I wanted to cry, but could not, so things would only be turning around for the better.

Only a few tears or so, I promise. Of course, I would miss her, but I was rational enough to know what was wrong. Some things were not to last, and every ending presented itself with the possibility to conduct new beginnings. I thought about Alice back in the bookstore, and her face came back to me. I knew I liked her; I really did and thought this was an opportunity for something new. Every ending is a chance for renewal.

Things could have been different if I never met Alice. Laura may not have been scared or doubted the integrity of my character. Our conversations were honest, no doubt, but never completely so because we cannot help but hide things from ourselves. I wished that things did not necessarily turn out like this, due to events beyond my control, but there is no escaping that, in many ways, or perhaps in all ways, we are formed outside of us.

***

I met Jack in the nearest café, and he told me what he had done.

'You know, I took him on.'

'And?'

'I won; I can't believe I did it. Yeah, turns out the higher administration was always against him, and they don't like crazy bosses like those.'

He walked around and waited.

'What about you?'

'Yeah, Laura and I broke up. Well, before we could get divorced.'

He laughed.

'You know what I find so funny in us?'

'Go on.'

'In the Service, we have to deal with major issues. Modern slavery, people starving through lack of benefits, potential violence. But here we are talking about problems, yes issues, but nothing that the rest of the world have had to go through. Why are we doing this?'

'We have to. I mean as friends and as people. Friendship is all about honesty and trust.

'Vulnerability. And something always has to be rainy, for us to enjoy the sun.'

'Well, let's drink to that. To first world problems.'

'Class.'

'It feels a bit disrespectful, though, laughing at everything.'

'I think that when someone is laughing about something, at least someone is happy.'

'Fair enough.'

'There is no point in hiding from the problems that we all face. So it's good to have inconsequential troubles than profoundly disturbing ones. And there is no way out of that.'

I zoomed out and looked at the whole world at large. Even the biggest of wars were nothing more than the exploits of a myriad of ants, and the things I had and believed were scarcely more than the dividends of what was a good life but maybe lacked meaning.

Still, despite this lack, I was joyous and thanked God that of all the bizarre and diverse places on this Earth that, for now, I was in a garden city.

Grant me the serenity to accept the things I cannot change, the courage to change the things that I can, and the wisdom to know the difference.

—Reinhold Niebuhr